Szymon Symanski
Goes to Hell

Lloyd Dobbins Jr.

D1518463

Chapter 1: The Barista

Szymon Symanski was a simple man, but he was complicated. Like a Rubick's cube. Or Dungeons & Dragons. Or filing taxes. Or using Saran Wrap. He was a taxpayer. He bought girl scout cookies. He occasionally went to the gym. He even donated to toys for tots. But he was also a serial killer. Well, a hitman. There's so much difference. "Oh I get paid." Yeah, Yeah, Yeah, Szymon. And he was a cultist. Ever hear of C'thulu? Yeah he was Szymon's big daddy. His reason to live.

Szymon was once told that C'thulu was present at a ritual, but that he would only appear if there was an orgy; several of the attendees were against an orgy for varying reasons: age, color, shape, size, etc...so the orgy didn't happen and nobody saw C'thulu. Go figure. People are so picky. Szymon was only picky about two things: ice cream and sex. He liked rocky road and men. But not in that order.

On Friday, May 13th, Szyman's life changed forever. It started out the same as any other day. He showered, shaved, and fried himself an ostritch egg. Over medium of course. And he placed the leftovers in the fridge, in a Tupperware container with a pink lid. He always fed his leftovers to the stray cats at dinner time.

Once he was fully dressed (aside from his hairy feet) in his cardigan sweater and Hagar slacks, with his rainbow suspenders tightly stretched to his narrow shoulders, Szymon began his morning stroll to the nearby cafe. Szymon didn't wear shoes because he

1

wanted to feel the earth. He wanted to be connected to the mother of all things. Also, a woman with a foot fetish once told him he had the most masculine feet she had ever seen. Flaunt it if you've got it.

When Szymon arrived at the cafe, he noticed through the front window that his usual barista was not in his usual place. There was a new guy. "Oh no, this can't be happening. What about my routine?" thought Szymon. "Big Richard makes my coffee. He always makes my coffee. This will not stand." Despite his dismay, Szymon entered the cafe. Once the door closed behind him, the new guy said, "Welcome to the Evergreen Cafe. What can i get you this fine morning?"

"Well, you can start by getting me Big Richard."

"My apologies, sir, but Richard doesn't work here anymore."

"What? He said nothing to me about quitting."

"Yeah, his mother became ill, so he moved to North Dakota to take care of her."

"But I saw him Wednesday. He moved in two days?"

"It would seem so, sir."

"Don't call me sir. I work for a living."

"Sorry, dude."

"That's better. So, can you make a triple mocha frappuccino? Or should I go elsewhere?"

"I can and will, dude. But next time you come in here barefooted I'll be forced to ask you to leave. Health codes, you know."

Szymon's face went red as he carefully examined this young man with his picture-perfect hair, healthy skin, cute button nose, sturdy jaw, and athletic physique. "You're a fine specimen," Szymon thought. Then he said, "I will excuse your insubordination just this once, young man."

"Ha ha, you're adorable. What name am I putting on the cup?"

"Szymon. That's S...Z--"

"I know how to spell Simon," interrupted the new guy.

So Szymon waited patiently, and when he received his coffee, "Simon" was written on the side of the cup with a Sharpie. S-I-M-O-N. Simon. Szymon (S-Z-Y-M-O-N) was infuriated. And then he noticed that the new guy had dotted the "I" with a heart. Szymon was overwhelmed by perplexedness. Why a heart? First, Szymon thought, "Why didn't my gaydar go off?" Then he thought, "Even if he does like men, doesn't he realize I'm his grandfather's age?" And then he thought, "He's obviously just razzing me. Fucking Gen-Z and their pranks--their goddamn social experiments. Well, this old fart ain't fallin' for it, I tell you."

At that moment, the new guy flashed a sideways grin at Szymon and said, "By the way, You can call me Ernest."

"Like Hemmingway."

"Like who?"

"Forget it."

"Well, anyways, have a great day. I have a feeling I'll be seeing a lot of you."

As Szymon exited the cafe, he thought, "Unbelievable. I live in a world where people don't know Hemmingway. Where did we go wrong?"

When Szymon finished his coffee, he prepared for work. First, he put on his gun harness. Then he loaded two Desert Eagle Mark XIX's and slid them into the holsters. Lastly, he donned his favorite black hooded cloak and locked the front door of his mobile home on the way out. In the driveway, Szymon's 1958 Cadillac hearse waited to go to work, which it did while blowing people's minds on the way. It was in cherry condition. It was both spooky and gorgeous. It was marvelous.

On his way to work, Szymon passed a mother with her small child. The little girl opened her mouth in awe of Martha, the jet-black hearse, with the creepy old man at the helm. The woman covered her daughter's eyes as though the whole scene was a pornographic film. Szymon then parallel parked in front of a dry cleaners. He disembarked his creepy vessel and walked to the shop with sea legs making it difficult to walk (just kidding, he walked funny because he was old).

He entered the dry cleaners and the stupid bell rang. Then he said, "Pick up for Jones." The fifty-something year old Korean woman who ran the cleaners was standing idly behind the counter as though she had no legitimate work to do. She was wearing a basketball jersey, with a big gold and diamond encrusted dollar sign hanging from her neck.

"Ah yes. Jones. One moment." The woman grabbed a black garment bag off the rack, where it was in the front, alone, as though she was expecting him. "Can i see your ticket?" asked the woman.

Szymon flashed her the paper stub and said, "Here you are."

"Thank you. Did you see the game last night, dawg? That shit was unreal!"

"You know i don't own a television, Mrs. Kim."

"Oh yeah. I don't understand. It's not like you can't afford it."

"I can't afford the loss of brain cells, Mrs. Kim."

"Blah. Brain cells are over-rated, Mr. Jones." replied Mrs. Kim.

"Ha, it was a pleasure as always, Mrs. Kim."

Szyman returned to his car and carefully placed the garment bag on the passenger seat. Once he was seated, he closed his door and unzipped the garment bag. First he pulled out two neatly-banded stacks of money (one was half his pay for the last job

5

and the other was half his pay for the next job). He tossed them both in the glove box without counting them and reached into the bag to retrieve a manilla envelope. He spilled the contents into his lap and instantly a black and white photograph stopped his heart for a moment. It was Ernest from the cafe.

Szymon stared blankly and then pounded three times on the steering wheel. "Oh curses. Curses, curses, curses." muttered Szymon. In over forty years of being a hired assassin, he had never had to kill someone he had already met. Thinking about it now, he realized it was probably against the odds that such was true. Even so, he now had to figure out what to do about it. He couldn't see Ernest as just a mark because he met him as a person. But he couldn't pass on the job because Mrs. Kim would be furious and might not give him any more jobs. This was going to take some serious contemplation, so Szymon drove to his thinking spot.

When Szymon got to the Jefferson canal, he grabbed a bag of bread from the passenger side floorboard and exited his car. The canal was the only one in Anywhere, Oregon, where Szymon lived. It was only five or six blocks long and was parallel to the numbered streets downtown. Szymon liked the canal because he loved feeding the ducks.

No sooner than Szymon reached the bank, an American black duck hurriedly swam towards him. Szymon tossed it a few small pieces of bread and relaxed. "Hello, Daffy," Szymon said to the duck. Other ducks in the canal noticed the bread being shared and surrounded Daffy; they were mostly mallards. Szymon attempted to hit Daffy with the pieces of bread so that he might have a better chance of eating them first.

"So, Daffy. What am I gonna do about the kid at the cafe? Sure, the smart-mouth little punk was a bit annoying, but he doesn't deserve to die for that reason alone. Why does the Korean mafia want him dead anyway? He's not even old enough to drink at the bar. He's just a kid. I guess he's not so bad. He sure is gorgeous. But, I'm close to retirement, Daffy, and I'm not messing that up over a new acquaintance. I guess I can ask him what he did before I make a decision. Thanks, Daffy. I knew you'd help me figure it out."

According to the file Mrs. Kim gave Szymon, Ernest McKenzie got off work at 3, worked out at the gym until 5, visited his grandmother until 7, then picked up some food and drove home to eat dinner. When Ernest made it to his apartment, Szymon was waiting in the living room. When Ernest flipped on the lights, he noticed Szymon sitting in his recliner holding two Desert Eagles.

"Szymon Symanski, with a 'Z' and two 'Y's'. Is that Polish?"

"How do you know my name?"

"I looked you up on Google. Did you know u have an outstanding parking ticket? You better take care of that."

"Enough of this nonsense. Why does the Korean mafia want you dead?"

"Beats the hell out of me. I don't associate with the mob."

"Well do you know any Koreans?"

"My ex-fiance is Korean. You don't think he put a hit out for me?"

"Maybe. But most likely it was a relative."

"Well remind me never to date a Korean."

"How can you be so casual?"

"How am I supposed to be? You want me to grovel? I'm not afraid of death. I believe in reincarnation. So, go ahead. Maybe I'll come back as a butterfly."

"This is serious. If I don't kill you, they might put a hit out on me. Please respect the significance of this situation."

"Ok. I feel for you, Pops. But do you have a choice in the matter?"

Szymon hesitated to reply. "Well, I suppose not."

"Then get it over with."

"No, goddamnit! I can't do it." As Szymon stared at Ernest's beautiful face, his eyes became watery. "I'll speak with the boss tomorrow. Maybe I can work something out."

"Damn, Szymon. You're a big softy."

"Watch your mouth, youngster. I'll be in touch. Just carry on as usual. Pretend you know nothing."

"That shouldn't be too hard."

"Always with the jokes this kid."

"By the way, what's with the robe? Are you a wizard or something?"

"Bah! I'm done here."

Szymon left and went to his favorite diner for supper. He felt it easier to think in a public setting for some reason. He had the usual: chicken-fried steak and a short-stack of pancakes with blackberry syrup. While eating, Szymon decided he would ask Mrs. Kim if there was any way Ernest could pay retribution for breaking the young man's heart. Then he returned home to feed the stray cats.

When Szymon opened the front door, he saw Ernest, limp and lifeless on the floor with one of Szymon's many pistols in his hand. He lied on his back with his shirt unbuttoned. On his chest was carved, "You're Welcome," with a sharp blade.

"Oh God! What have you done, Ernest?"

Chapter 2: The Ritual

Szymon Szymanski was a mess. What caliber of mess was he? He was dog diarrhea on the Persian rug. Szymon was also a wreck. What caliber of wreck was he? He was a school bus full of highly gifted children barreling into a jack-knifed semi-truck hauling rocket fuel.

At least he wasn't alone. He had his good friend--well, his only friend--Hank. Luckily, when Szymon called, Hank was only on his second beer. Hank had a strict rule: no operating heavy machinery, firearms, or kitchen appliances after beer three.

"What's up, Szymon?"

"I need you to help me feed the fish."

"Sure thing, Szymon. Need me to bring any heat?"

"Nope."

After he got off the phone, Hank immediately set his wrench on his toolbox, locked up the garage, grabbed a Louisville slugger that was leaning on the side of the garage and mounted his trusty steed, a 2012 Harley Davidson Road King.

When he got to Szymon's trailer, Hank said, "Fuck, I hate fish," and reluctantly went inside. On the back of his leather was a Harley Davidson patch. On the front was embroidered, Hanky Panky.

As Hank opened the door, he yelled, "Szymon."

When he stepped inside, he saw Ernest's body on the floor with his shirt buttoned up, and, instead of cursing, he loudly exclaimed, "Damn, your boyfriend sure is handsome."

"Was. He was handsome. But he wasn't my boyfriend." Szymon entered the living room as he spoke. "What about you? Does Hanky Panky have a girlfriend these days?"

After a pause, Hank said, "Holy shit. That's so weird. I felt like you were only asking me that to let an invisible audience know that I date women."

"Uhhhhhhhhhhhhh, what? Have you been eating peyote?"

"No, I haven't been eating peyote. I just feel like we're characters in a story, man."

"You've been eating peyote. Now help me with this body."

Lifting Ernest's body was easy enough, and they had little trouble in big China--I mean little difficulty--carrying the body into the spare bedroom, where a giant five-foot-tall fish tank filled most of the room. They set the body down on a stretcher with a harness attached to an electric over-head crane. That's when one of the fish (Pygocentrus Nattereri to be exact) swam headfirst into the glass and sent Hank back a few feet.

"Fuck, man! Why do you have piranhas? Why can't you just bury bodies in the desert like a normal

12

person?"

"What desert?" Szymon used the crane's control to lift the body to the ceiling and move it over the tank.

"That's beside the point. The point I'm making is that--Holy Jesus Fuck! How long have you been starving these little bastards, man?"

The vicious carrion-feeders swarmed the body as it was lowered, and a reddish pink cloud erupted in the water.

"If you're out of food, you can always feed them your beloved alley cats."

"Hey. Watch your mouth, Hanky."

"Ok. Ok. So, your silence is killing me. What's the deal with the kid you just fed to fucking piranhas?"

"We just fed to piranhas. You're an accessory. And he was the new guy at the cafe. And he's my mark."

"Your mark? Then what the fuck is he doing here? You never touch the corpses."

"He said he looked me up on Google, whatever that means."

"What? Why? Why did he google you? What all did he know?"

Szymon told Hank the entire story. When he

was done, Hank laughed like he had just hit his funny bone on something and didn't want to laugh but wanted to laugh but didn't want to laugh. Then he took a sip of coffee and returned the mug to the short table between him and Szymon, where they sat on Lazy Boy's in the living room."

"That wasn't the craziest shit I've ever heard, but it sure was a doozy. You should write that shit down. You could sell it as a novella--so you don't blow your cover."

"Oh, shut up, Hank."

"No, I'm serious. Well, at least it all worked out. The kid took your secrets to the grave--or the fish bellies--and your boss will pay you tomorrow for killing a kid who killed himself. It's airtight, man. Yet you seem worried about something. What is it?"

"I'm worried about my soul, Hank."

"Your soul? But you don't give a shit about that. Aren't you a C'thulite or whatever it's called?"

"Yes, but I'm technically still Jewish. So, I kinda believe in an after-life."

"You're still hung up on that kid?"

"Yes, he tried to do me a favor and now, if Hell (or Gehenna) exists, he's probably there in endless agony. Because of me."

"Oh, Jesus, Szymon. He was probably bound for Hell anyway, eventually. He was a peter-puffer.

14

You've sent countless people to Hell pre-maturely. What's different about this kid?"

"Well, that's the first thing. He was a kid. But the fact that he did it for me carries a lot of weight as well."

"Well, that sucks, Szymon, but I don't think there's anything you can do about it. Can i get you some more coffee?"

Deep in thought, Szymon nodded.

"You take sugar?"

"No thank you, Hanky. I'm sweet enough."

The next morning, Szymon woke up, but he didn't shower. And he didn't shave. And he didn't fry himself an ostrich egg. And, instead of going to the cafe, he brewed a pot of Columbian roast. While it brewed, Szymon got dressed, with his handsome black yarmulke on his head. He then put a splash of cold water in his cup so he could drink his coffee faster than usual. When his cup was empty, he donned his black cloak (no guns today) and drove to the synagogue, where he hoped to get some answers. Since it was Saturday (Shabbat), services would be held in the morning. That is why Szymon got up early, so he could speak to the Rabbi before he was busy addressing the congregation. When Szymon got there, it was still easy to find parking, and the Rabbi was at the front doors, welcoming the early birds (mostly elderly women).

"Good morning, Szymon. It's unusual to see

you here. Is there something I can do for you? Answer some questions perhaps?"

"Yes, questions. I need answers, Rabbi."

"Answers I may have. Shall we go to my office?"

"Yes, Rabbi. That would be great."

The Rabbi's office was small enough to be considered modest but large enough to convey that the rabbi deserved respect. It was heavily decorated, with tapestries and framed degrees and certificates on the walls, a menorah on the bookshelf next to a teddy bear with a Yarmulke on its head, and on the desk was a mess of little figurines including a Moses bobble-head that caught Szymon's eye.

"Ok, Szymon. What's your first question?"

"Well, I was wondering if Gehenna actually exists."

"Oh, I see. Well, you may know that Gehenna is a topic we Jews don't all exactly agree on. I believe Gehenna exists. And that it's a place of torture for those who broke the commandments. And I believe the punishment lasts for up to 12 months, and then you're whisked away and sent to Gan Eden to await the arrival of the Messiah. But that's not the only theory. My parents don't believe in Gehenna at all. Although, my father wishes he did, so that he could eventually get more than a minute away from my mother. And my brother believes Gehenna is eternal. He believes the righteous and the wicked all go to Sheol to wait to be judged and then sent to either Gan Eden or Gehenna for the rest of time."

"So, if it exists, it's either 12 months or eternity? Ok. That's a big difference."

"What's your second question?"

"Well, Rabbi, someone I knew killed himself recently, and I was wondering if he automatically went to Gehenna."

"Oh. Sorry for your loss." The Rabbi lightly touched Szymon's hand, where it rested on the desk, with the fingers of one hand. "Well, murder is a commandment and results in punishment, and suicide is self-murder. So, I'd think he's in or on his way to Gehenna, unfortunately."

"Ok, thanks for your help, Rabbi."

"No problem, Szymon. But there is something you could do for me. I heard you take care of people. I want you to take care of my wife."

"Oh. Uh, no, I don't think it's wise to mix business and religion. I'm sorry, Rabbi."

"You sure? I'll pay well."

"I'm sure, Rabbi."

"I'll throw in that Moses bobble-head you've had your eye on. It's a collector's item."

"No, I'd rather not, Rabbi."

"Ok, no problem. It was worth a shot."

After leaving the synagogue, Szymon drove to the occult shop, aptly named, Odetta's Oddities. Odetta was standing at the register when Szymon entered the shop. She was a robust black woman with a bandana on her head like a gypsy. The shop contained anything and everything a dirty, Pagan hippie might spend their money on, from patchouli oil to goat's blood.

"Hello, Szymon. What can I do for you?"

"Do you have any books that explain how to get someone out of Hell?"

"Well...you know, I think I have one that should. One moment. Odetta flew down the rows of shelves and returned momentarily holding a large, thick, black book with a red pentagram on the cover.

"Here. According to the index, it's on page 666." Odetta searched for the page and said, "Ok, it says the only way to get someone out of Hell is to go to hell, find Satan, and trade your soul for the other person's."

"Oh ok. I guess that means I've got to kill myself."

"Oh Lord," said Odetta.

"Odetta, can i use your rest room?"

"Uh."

"To urinate. I'm not gonna kill myself...yet. I have a few things to do first."

Among those things were paying the lot rent on his trailer and making sure Hank was listed as sole heir of his estate in his will. When he was finished performing these tasks, he asked himself if there was anything else he needed to do before shuffling off this mortal coil. "Mmm, nope. I guess I'm ready to bite the bullet."

But, Szymon was pretty nervous about killing the last person he ever thought he would have to kill. So, he stopped at the liquor store for some liquid courage. As he wandered down the aisles perusing the shelves in search of something appealing, he passed the cooler containing wines and cocktails and such that are served chilled. That's when he spotted his favorite Saki in it's large blue bottle labeled, Moonstone Asian Pear in yellow letters. "Well, what the Hell? Saki it is."

After Szymon drove home, he called Hank on his land-line and told him he needed his help with something, but that he couldn't tell him what it was. Hank asked when and where, and Szymon replied, "Now would be great, but whenever you can get over to my trailer would work just fine." When Hank got to Szymon's, Szymon was already partially buzzed from the Saki he held in his hand.

"What the Hell, Szymon? You don't drink. What's the occasion?"

19

"I'm going to Hell, Hanky."

"Yeah, we probably all are. What's your point?"

"No, I'm going there today, Hank."

"What? And what's with the kimono?"

"Seppuku, Hank."

"What? First of all, why? And secondly, you aren't Japanese."

"I trained there when I was young. Didn't I ever tell you that?"

"So. You're still not Japanese."

"That's not important, Hank. What is important is that you are here to witness my most honorable death." Szymon took a big swallow of sake and belched immediately.

"Why? And don't you dare say it's because of that kid."

"Of course it's about the kid. I'm gonna save him, Hank."

"Damnit Szymon. He's not your responsibility."

"Hey! I'll say what, or who, isn't or isn't--is--my responsibility, thank you very much." Szymon stumbled over to a mat that was spread out in the center of the room. It was white to match his kimono. On it rested a tanto, a Samurai knife traditionally used for seppuku.

"Just so you know, Szymon, I'm not chopping your head off, so don't even ask."

"That's fine. I don't need your help. I just need you to watch."

"This is crazy, Szymon. How do you expect to save him? You gonna just waltz in and find him and sneak him out the back door?"

"I'm going to make a deal with the devil, Hank."

"What you got that would interest the devil, Szymon?"

"My soul. I have 4,017 confirmed kills, Hank. I'm sure I can make a deal."

"Ok, sure. That might work. But what about your life savings and your retirement? If you do this, it means you worked your whole life for nothing."

"Uhhh, so what...Well, that's not true anyway. I left it all to you."

"Left what to me?"

"My will. I left it all to you."

"What? Don't you have family to leave it to?"

"No, my family disowned me years ago."

"Oh, yeah, for being gay."

"No, they thought i killed the uncle who

molested me."

"Did you?"

"Well, yeah. Wouldn't you?"

"You make a valid point. So, everything. Does that include the car and the trailer?"

"Everything, Hank. Including the fish you love so much."

"Gee, thanks, Szymon, but those fuckers are getting sold."

"They're yours. Do whatever you want." Szymon took another big gulp of Saki and wiped his mouth with the back of his hand. Then, he kneeled on the mat with his butt resting on his feet. Szymon set the bottle down, and it fell over, spilling its remaining contents on the carpet. "Party foul." Szymon laughed boisterously.

"Damnit, Szymon. I don't think you're sober enough to do this right."

"Oh, poppycock. How hard can it be to slice your belly open? It's not exactly rocket surgery, Hank." Szymon picked up the knife with one hand and opened his kimono with the other. That's when Hank spoke abruptly.

"Wait. This is your last chance to back out of this, Szymon."

"Oh, stop being such a pussy, Hank."

22

"Ok. It's your life."

"Damn right it's my life."

Szymon took a deep breath and thrust the knife into the left side of his abdomen. As he did so, Hank watched the pain wash over Szymon's face. Szymon took another deep breath and then, with both hands, pulled the blade across to the other side of his abdomen with all the force he could muster. His glossy, wide-open eyes resembled fisheyes as his intestines spilled out onto the mat. "Fuck, fuck, fuck, fuck, fuck. It hurts."

Hank pulled his pistol and asked, "You want me to shoot you in the head?"

Breathing heavily, his voice weak and empty, Szymon answered, "No, Hank. That will ruin the ritual. Just let me suffer."

Szymon closed his eyes and meditated on his current goal. He pictured Ernest smiling with his arms out, offering him a hug for coming to his rescue. A few moments of pure agony transpired and then Szymon fell over on his side. His consciousness faded to nothingness before his head reached the floor. Hank watched helplessly and then, wringing his sweaty palms nervously, he said, "Well, I guess it's my job to call the police. Great. Should probably wait for him to bleed out though. I'd hate for them to resuscitate him only for him to have to do it again."

Chapter 3: The Weigh-station

When Szymon gained consciousness, he was lying on the floor of an elevator all alone. The elevator was moving, but he didn't know which direction it was going. Horrible music was playing from a speaker: some kind of orchestral, instrumental version of an unidentifiable pop song. The entirety of the elevator's interior was a dark gray, and there were no buttons or floor indicator as far as Szymon could tell. As he got to his feet, he felt his abdomen and found that his body was whole. He was, however, still wearing the blood-soaked kimono. Well, the blood had dried, but you get the drift.

"I wonder which way I'm going," Szymon thought. "Down. It's gotta be down. Listen to this God-forsaken music. There's no land of white clouds and golden palaces awaiting me past this door. You can be sure of that."

That's when the elevator came to a stop, and the door slid open, revealing a vast expanse of dark gray. The walls, the floor, and the ceiling were all nothing other than a dark gray finish, as though it was all some sort of polished metal. Szymon could hardly see it with the lack of color contrast, but there was a dark gray reception desk of sorts in the distance ahead of him.

Szymon approached the desk, and, as he did, a dark-haired woman became visible behind it. "Well, if this isn't ominous, I don't know what is," Szymon said to himself. When he reached the desk, Szymon

25

stopped and waited for the woman, who was reading a paperback novel, to acknowledge his existence. On the cover of the novel, was printed "Szymon Symanski Goes to Hell." When Szymon read the title, he was startled (naturally).

"So this is Hell?" Szymon thought. "Seems underwhelming." As though she had "heard" her cue, the dark-haired woman quickly set down her book, revealing the most hideous face Szymon had ever seen: something straight out of a horror movie. Her skin had been removed somehow, from her chin to her eyes, where her horn-rimmed glasses rested on her skinless nose. Maggots were eating at the flesh, and suddenly a large cockroach skittered out of her ear, jumped to the counter-top, and gained its bearing just before the woman smashed it quickly with her hand. When she raised her hand to her mouth, presumably to lick it, Szymon turned away.

When Szymon turned, he saw that a small black man wearing a finely tailored, gray suit, and holding a lit cigar, was standing there--had been standing behind him for who knows how long.

"Actually, Szymon, this is not Hell. It's more like Sheol, if you want to call it that. We call it The Weigh Station."

"Holy shit! Sammy Davis Jr? Is that really you?"

"Yeah, it's me. The only black, Puerto Rican, one-eyed, Jewish entertainer in the universe, baby."

"What's the deal with this lady, Sammy?" As

26

szymon spoke, he turned to find that the woman and the desk were no longer there. "Where'd she go?"

"Same place she came from, Szymon. Nowhere."

"Excuse me?"

"Nothing actually exists here. You just see what you wanna see. I don't even exist. I'm only here because you want me here, Szymon. So...shall we go to Hell now?"

"Wait a second, Sammy. Aren't you gonna show me some moves?"

"Oh...no. I couldn't. I'm sorry Szymon, but I don't dance anymore. I retired my tap shoes for good, my man."

"That's a shame. I'm sorry to hear that, Sammy."

"It's all gravy, baby. Shall we?"

Sammy puffed on his Cuban cigar and headed toward the elevator that Szymon arrived in. As Szymon followed closely behind, his head was swimming with questions. "Why would Sammy Davis Jr. quit dancing?" he thought. "Something serious must've happened."

"Sammy, I thought Sheol was where people awaited judgement. Why didn't I have to wait?"

"But you did. Time works differently here, Szymon. All three realms of the after-life exist in a

27

separate dimension outside of time and space."

They entered the elevator and turned around as the door slid shut.

"You see, Szymon? Everyone who ever died or ever will die arrived at different times but also at the same time. This is the end of time."

"But I didn't see anybody else."

"No-one does. Can you imagine what kind of mad-house this would be if they did?"

"That's a good point. But, what about Hell? Is it the same way?"

"Oh, no. All the sinners are crammed together in Hell. It's supposed to be a mad-house."

"I see. Hey, Sammy. What's with this God-awful music?"

"It's elevator music, Szymon. It's supposed to be bad. Also, it freaks out the righteous because they assume they must be headed to Hell. Hilarious. We like to have fun here."

"O.K."

"Anymore questions before we get there and I have to say adieu?"

"Yeah, is my uncle, Bernard, here by chance?"

"The child-fucker who raped you? Yeah, he's in the 9th Circle, and still a tremendously wicked dude."

28

"The 9th Circle? So, Dante was right?"

"Of course he was. What? You thought that story was a fabrication?"

"Well, yeah."

"Well, you thought wrong, my man."

"Ok. So, is that where I'm going: The 9th Circle?"

"Couldn't tell ya, Szymon. That's out of my jurisdiction. You know I would if I could. Well, this is where I say goodbye, Szymon. Don't be a square, baby."

Sammy Davis Jr. disappeared and Szymon said to himself, "Real or not, I just met Sammy Davis Jr., baby." The elevator stopped and the door slid open, revealing a small waiting room, entirely painted red, with a red desk in the middle, red plastic chairs lining the walls, and red shag carpeting covering the floor. Behind the short desk stood what appeared to be an imp, with a long face, long nose, long chin, long ears, and long horns that protruded mostly to the front before curving upward. "His" skin was (you guessed it) red.

There was a 50-inch television mounted in one corner, near the ceiling. On three of the chairs sat "people," two of which were human. The third was an extra-terrestrial from Planet Nixmar, but of course Szymon didn't know that. He also didn't know that they were a hermaphrodite, as were nearly all the members of their species. They were a gelatinous, green cube, and did not need legs, for they could levitate at any height. They also did not need arms, for they possessed telekinetic powers. Both humans were female, one from India, the other from Midland City, Indiana. Standing in front of the elevator was Sammy Davis Jr., wearing a red suit, and still smoking a Cuban cigar.

"What in the Hell?"

"Indeed, Szymon. Welcome to Jewish Hell. Would you like a pickle?" A large jar of kosher dills appeared in Sammy's hands.

"Jewish Hell? So Gehenna really exists?"

"No, I'm just fucking with you, Szymon. This is regular Hell. The only Hell. One universe, one Hell. Pickle?"

"No, I'm not hungry."

"Suit yourself."

The jar of pickles disappeared and Szymon showed a degree of alarm on his face.

"Wait a second. How can you control reality in Hell? Unless you're..."

"Unless what, Szymon? Unless I'm fucking Lucifer? You bore me with your naivete."

"Damnit. I knew something was rotten in Denmark when you didn't want to dance. You probably can't dance, can you, asshole?"

"You forget your place, Szymon. This is my kingdom. You will show me respect."

"I will do no such thing, big fella. I have come here with one purpose."

"Yeah, yeah, yeah. To trade your soul for the soul of your beloved Ernest. Well, I hate to break it to you, Szymon, but it's not going to be that easy."

"Then what? What must I do?"

"You must face your sins, Szymon. All nine of them. If you can make it to the 9th Circle without losing your mind, only then will I discuss the possibility of releasing your boyfriend."

"He's not my boyfriend."

"Oh, save it for the imps, Szymon. They might be stupid enough to believe that bullshit."

"So, what now? You gonna show me your true form? You gonna try to frighten me?"

"Frighten you? There's no need. You'll do that to yourself, Szymon, in due time."

As Lucifer vanished, his words echoed in Szymon's head.

"Is that it?" Szymon shouted. "Is that really all you're going to tell me? But what do I do next? How do I get to the 9th Circle?"

Then Szymon thought, "Wait a second. If the nine circles exist, then Sheol does not. That means what he said about time might also be a lie. And that would mean much of my family is here waiting for me. This should be fun."

"Excuse me. Mr. Imp, is this the 1st Circle?"

"No, it's the 13th triangle. Huh huh. Dumbass."

"Well, what am I supposed to do now?"

"Uh, duh. Sit down and wait for your case-worker to call your name. Dumbass."

Chapter 4: Reception

Immediately, Szymon took a long look at his new surroundings. The Indian woman was young and wore an elaborate red dress, with a red bindi between her eyes, and a nose ring connected to her left earing by an exquisite, gold chain that hung next to her mournful frown. Szymon knew enough about her culture to realize that she must have died on her wedding night. "What a shame," thought Szymon. Her tears stung him right in the soul.

The Hoosier woman from the great state of Indiana, in the good ole U.S. of A., wore a simple brown dress with a white apron, and a white bonnet. The dress and apron were badly burned by flames, revealing her legs and bits of her hand-sewn underwear and bra-less breasts. Her long blonde hair was badly singed.

On the Television played an episode of The Twilight Zone that Szymon had seen at least once. The two women were watching the show as attentively as they could, probably to keep their minds distracted. There were no subtitles and Szymon thought, "That's not fair."

"Hey, Mr. Imp. You think you could turn on Hindi subtitles so this woman can understand what they're saying?"

The Indian woman interrupted him in English, saying, "It's in Hindi. And you are also speaking Hindi. So what's the problem?"

33

"No, I'm speaking English. So are you."

Irritated, the imp said, "Would you people shut up? There's only one language in Hell. Duh."

Szymon's mind was a tesla coil on fire in an earthquake on a small island with an active volcano, as nuclear bombs went off everywhere as far as the eye could see. His mind was fucked. First he thought, "Hell should be easier to traverse if I can understand what everybody's saying." Next he thought, "This means I can speak to that alien." Then he thought, "Holy fuck. Was that girl burned at the stake?"

"Excuse me miss, but what year did you die?

"2023. Why?"

"Where are you from?"

"A small community outside Midland City."

"Do you mind if I ask how you died?"

The woman stammered with a quivering voice as she spoke, "I was burned alive, sir."

"For what? Surely not for being a witch."

"Yes, sir. Witch, sir."

According to Google, "The last trial of a woman accused of witchcraft and executed by burning was not in Doruchow, Poland in Wielkopolski Province in 1776 – as commonly accepted – but 34 years later in August 1811. This happened in the city of Reszel in Warmia

Province. The last victim to be burnt at the stake was Barbara Zdunk."

They apparently haven't heard about Helena Duncan yet.

"Well, why on Earth would anyone think you were a witch?" asked Szymon as he sat down next to the Hoosier woman.

"For having intercourse, sir," answered Helena Duncan.

"For having sex? What?"

"With someone other than Reverend Joe, sir."

"Oh, what's their name?"

"Billy Brindler."

"Do you love Billy?"

"With my whole heart, sir."

"That's nice. That's really beautiful. Well, they'll find you. Eventually. Don't lose hope. Hope is a snowflake in Hell...Oh shit, um..." Szymon froze.

"It's ok. Please continue," urged the young blonde woman.

"...um, hope is a badass snowflake in hell--with Mr. Freeze's freeze gun--that can survive hell as long as it believes in itself."

"Thank you, sir. Those were nice words. But

Billy won't find me on Venus. So I'll never see him again."

"Wait. What? Venus?"

"It's where New Venutians go when they die."

"Then why aren't you there?"

"Because I'm a witch, sir."

"You're not a witch."

"According to the Newish Order of the New Venutians, I am a witch and have been sent to Hell accordingly."

"Well, I don't know if I should believe him, but Lucifer said, 'One Universe, one Hell.' So, does your Hell have The 9 Circles?"

"I don't know, sir."

"Well, shit. Well, I don't think you're a witch."

"If she wants to be a witch, let her be a witch," interrupted the gelatinous green cube in a high-pitch, electronic-sounding voice.

"Oh! You got some balls telling me what i can and can't do (in Hell). Do you even have balls? Can I see them? Am I looking at them right now?"

Using their mind, the Nixmarian lifted Szymon out of his seat and threw him across the room, slamming him into one of the red walls. Szymon stood, grunting.

"You'll pay for that."

Still wearing a blood-stained kimono, Szymon placed his palms together and harnessed his ki, focusing it into his hands. His hands lit light blue and he reached both hands down to his left side and drew a katana, which was surrounded by a glowing blue aura, out of an invisible sheath. He then stepped toward the Nixmarian.

"Diced or sliced?"

Szymon froze in his tracks as his body surged w/ electricity.

"A taser?" Szymon asked incredulously.

"Don't make me have to set it to lethal, dumbass."

"Ok, I give. Uncle. Uncle."

At that moment, the door opened and Sammy Davis Jr. stepped into the lobby wearing a black suit and smoking a Cuban cigar. "Helena Duncan? You're next."

The so-called witch stood and approached as Szymon's jaw dropped.

"Are you fucking kidding me? I'm ready for you this time, Big Fella," Szymon said, raising his sword."

"Oh, shoot. Did Lucifer pretend to be me again? That guy! He loves to joke. What can I say?"

"Are you serious? So, I don't have to kill you?"

"Kill me? Oh, heavens no. I'll show you some moves if you don't."

"Deal." Szymon slid his sword back into the invisible sheath and it disappeared entirely.

While Sammy danced, Szymon raised his arms and swiveled his hips in rhythm. Szymon could kill people, but he couldn't dance. Such is life (or death).

The desk imp couldn't resist an excuse to dance, so he immediately approached Helena Duncan to grind on her as she innocently enjoyed the attention.

When the dance was over, Szymon was heavily winded. Not sure exactly what he might find, Szymon felt his waist, searching for tools or implements that could serve useful on his journey. On his right hip, opposite the invisible sheath, hung a traditional, hand-made sake bottle tied to a braided strand of hemp rope. Szymon untied the bottle and swallowed a gulp of the finest substance he would ever imbibe.

"Hey, Szymon. I've gotta split, baby," said Sammy Davis Jr.

"Thanks for the dance, Sammy."

"No, thank you."

The young blonde "witch" shook Szymon's hand and he told her, "You got this, girl," before she and Sammy exited the door that Sammy had entered through.

"Well, she got Sammy Davis Jr.--the real one--as her case manager. I wonder who I'll get." Szymon glanced at the Nixmarian. They didn't move an inch. Szymon then sat next to the Indian woman, who was still crying. She hadn't flinched during the entire series of events.

"Sorry to pry, but why didn't you dance? Don't you like to dance?"

Before the woman could answer, the Nixmarian interjected. "Hey, Alpha-male. Why don't you just leave everyone alone? There is a perfectly good program on the monitor in the corner, and no-one is bothering you."

"You really think you can talk to me that way because you have magic powers? I have a sword. A very cool sword."

"You are only as strong as your tools, apeman."

"Oh, do you underestimate me?"

"You won't do anything. You are a coward."

"What? Because of that taser? I'm not afraid of a taser. That taser can't kill me. I'm already dead."

"Death? You know nothing of death. My oldest sibling convinced the entire population of Nixmar that ritual suicide was the only honorable way to atone for the shame that was brought on the entire species when a government scientist discovered that all of

39

Nixmar had been worshipping a Cocker Spaniel named Mitzy for millions of years. You see, a Polaroid photo of Mitzy had fallen out of God's pocket during the Big Bang and, when it was discovered, it was believed to be an image of the creator and was kept in the global museum. Anyway, the only reason I'm not in the 7th Circle with the rest of my people is that I refused to kill myself and was slain by my sibling. Don't worry, Earthling. I'll get my revenge."

"I don't mean to rain on your parade, but I really don't care if you get your revenge or not. And, just so you know, there's nothing wrong with ritual suicide. I mean, it hurts a little..."

"Oh, there you go again, pissing on the wrong tree."

"What do you know about trees?"

"Oh! You think Earth got all the trees? How arrogant."

Before Szymon could blurt out his retort, he was stopped by a loud cough.

"Szymon Symanski?"

Chapter 5: Limbo

Szymon turned his head to see a thin man with a white moustache and gray curls upon his head, with bits of white scattered about. He was tidy and comely, but a bit slumped over. He was wearing an orange v-neck sweater over a violet dress shirt and Szymon thought, "Somebody robbed Joker's closet."

"Aren't you Kurt Vonnegut?"

"In fact I am. So, tell me Szymon. What are you in here for?"

"Uh...well, I'm a hired killer, and there was this young man who--"

"I'm kidding. It's all in here." Kurt held up a thick paper file in a manilla folder and continued, "And, incidentally, it is also in here." He tapped the file on his head. "Read the whole thing twice. Please, Szymon, follow me."

The two exited the lobby, entering an immense cavern formed from a dull black stone of whatever sort. The cavern was slightly lit and Szymon looked up for a few seconds to see thousands of fireflies that were all glowing intermittently at different rhythms. Everywhere Szymon looked, he could see a round table being used for cards or dominos or a puzzle, or a t.v. surrounded by furniture full of people, or an imp with a medicine cart, handing out drugs and paper cups full of water. Szymon noticed that many of the people were wearing the traditional attire of non-Christian cultures.

41

Szymon crossed his eyes and exclaimed, "So this is Limbo? Well, this is just a giant nursing home."

"Isn't it great?" Kurt reached down and grabbed a paper cup full of pills and one full of water off a medicine cart.

"Hey, wait your turn, dumbass," said the imp pushing the cart. Kurt pointed to the name badge pinned to his sweater and looked back toward Szymon.

"Here, Szymon, try a blue one. They're to die for." Kurt handed Szymon the blue tablet and the cup of water, and gestured forward, beginning to walk. "I have to admit. I'm a big fan, Szymon. I especially like how you mailed yourself to the ruler of Abu Dhabi and escaped through the garbage chute after stabbing him through the eye socket to the frontal lobe with the letter opener he gave to himself as a coronation gift. Pure genius."

"Thanks, I guess. It's a real honor. I have a first edition copy of "Sirens of Titan" at my... Well, I did have a copy."

"Actually, if you had it in life, you have it in death. I know, just wait till the Christians find out about that. So, just reach into a pocket--oh you don't have pockets. Just reach inside that kimono and imagine you're pulling out that book."

Szymon did as Kurt directed, and pulled his copy of "Sirens of Titan" from inside his kimono.

"Oh, I love this book. Look. I signed your name

inside the cover, but nobody believed me. Damn, I love how this book encapsulates and also breaks down the notion that everything happens for a reason. I know, 'everything happens for a reason' is cheesy, but what about 'everything that happens causes or creates something good and something bad.' It's chaos, but there have to be rules. And if something caused something good to happen, it had a purpose, and a purpose is a reason."

"Oh," Kurt stared off into space for a moment and then shook his head and continued, "I just thought it was a book about a spaceman. But I like what you said."

Szymon laughed nervously and changed the subject. "It was really nice meeting you, Mr. Vonnegut, but I have an important mission. I hate to even wonder what Ernest is going through right now. I really must hurry."

"Oh yes. Ernest. The barista. Well, here's the deal, Szymon. The people downstairs know you're coming for them and directed me to keep an eye on you for your entire stay. So, whatever you do and wherever you go, you're stuck with me."

"Ok. Do You know the way to The 9th Circle?"

"Of a matter of fact, I do."

"Good, so what are we waiting for?"

"Well, there's someone I thought you might want to see. She's been waiting to talk to you."

"Oh no. Come on, Kurt. Please tell me you didn't sell me out."

"Trust me, Szymon. I'm doing you a favor. If you don't see her now, you may not get another chance."

"What? Is she gonna die again and go to Super Hell? And then die again and go to Mega Hell?"

"Come on, Szymon. You don't really think you can defeat Lucifer, do you?"

"What? Defeat him? But, it said in Odetta's book that all I had to do was trade my soul for Ernest's. Quid pro quo.

"You can't believe everything you read in a book, Szymon."

"What do you mean, defeat him? Can he be defeated?"

"Lucifer can in fact be defeated, technically. He must accept all challenges and must temporarily become mortal during the battle to the death to decide who will rule Hell."

"Rule Hell? Why would I want to do that?"

"Nearly infinite power. The only being you would have to answer to would be God, and he stays in the suburbs. You're in the slums. You'd be the slum lord. You'd have the best food, the best alcohol, the best weed, the best cigars, and as many sex slaves as you desire. Imagine."

"Oh, I'm imagining. You know what? Let's put a pin in that. We'll get back to it. Right now, where's my mother, so I can get this over with?"

"She should be right down there, Szymon."

Szymon saw some familiar faces in his peripheral vision and stopped in his tracks.

"Kurt, is that Mahatma Gandhi, Albert Einstein, and..."

"And Siddhartha Gautama."

"The original Buddha?"

"Yes. But please don't engage them. They will never let us get away from them."

"I just want to hear what they're talking about."

The three men were sitting around a table. Buddha and Gandhi were wearing robes. Einstein was wearing a custom-made black suit. Grinning like a cat that just killed a mouse, Einstein said, "I loved when Kim said she enjoyed what she does, and she wants her kids to grow up really loving what they do and finding their passion and figuring out how to make a business out of that. As if any of those kids will have a hard time making a career out of their passions. North's passion could be ventriloquism done with a puppet made from a taxidermized raccoon and she'd make millions of dollars doing it."

Gandhi replied, "Ha! Yeah, I loved when they

showed the old footage of Kris tripping and falling on her face in front of the paparazzi, and Kim yelling at them to delete the footage of her mom falling."

"Yes, that was priceless. But, my favorite part was when North came in wearing that jacket that was a size too big for her, and Kim said it belonged to North's father," said Buddha.

Einstein added, "Yeah, I love how Kanye gave the jacket to charity and then Kim found and bought it off the internet."

"She's such a hoarder!" exclaimed Buddha.

Kurt coughed to get Szymon's attention and said, "We should be going."

They started walking again.

"Are they talking about the Kardashians?" asked Szymon.

"I'm not sure what that is."

"It's a T.V. program I've heard about."

"Then probably. Those guys watch an awful lot of television. Here she is."

Szymon saw a petite yet plump woman, wearing a pink sweat suit, with pink curlers in her hair, sitting in a wooden rocking chair faced toward a television.

"Mother?"

Szymon's mother turned her head and smiled though her face looked like it had been lacquered with guilt. "Szymon, you came."

"Yes, Mother. You can thank Mr. Vonnegut for that."

"Please, call me Kurt."

"Thank you, Kurt."

"Mother, where is my father? Do you know?"

"Oh, your father. I'm so sorry I let him hurt you, Szymon."

Szymon's mind slipped down the rabbit hole. He was 7 and was sitting alone in the back seat of a powder blue Ford Galaxy with no seatbelt. His mother was driving. His father was drinking a beer. Szymon was playing with a rag doll. The year was 1965. When the song on the radio ended, a loud voice came out of the stereo speakers.

"Today, hostilities between India and Pakistan ended after a ceasefire was declared following American and Soviet intervention."

Szymon's father bent forward and yelled into the radio. "Fuck you, Lyndon B. Dickhead. You need to mind your own business. Let the towelheads kill each other. What do I care? What does this great nation care? We're not the world's babysitter."

"I don't know, honey," interjected Szymon's mother. "Voltaire said, 'With great power comes great responsibility.'"

Szymon's father quickly back-handed his wife across the face with his right hand and grabbed his beer from his left hand, where he had placed it temporarily. As he slapped her, he loudly stated, "Fuck what Voltaire said. Fuck Voltaire. If he was so fucking smart, why'd his parents name him Voltaire? Did he eat roadkill?"

When the hand had contacted Sandy Symanski's face, she had lost control of the steering wheel. She stomped on the brake pedal as the car had begun to veer. The car stopped abruptly, and Szymon's father dropped his beer in his lap. He immediately picked it up as foam continued to erupt from the opening.

"Learn to drive, woman!"

Szymon had caught himself on the back of the front seat. He sat back in his own seat and asked, "Why did you hurt Mommy?"

"Mind your own business, Junior. And give me that." Szymon Sr. grabbed the rag doll out of his son's hands and threw it out the window. "Boys who play with dolls grow up to be Lyndon B. Johnson."

Szymon snapped out of his daydream and said, "It's ok, Mother. Where is he? I need to talk to him."

"Szymon, don't worry about your father. He's paying for his crimes against humanity. But you. How are you in the First Circle? I know you killed your uncle.

48

What were the odds of 2 trained swordsmen being in the same small town at the same time?"

"It had to be done, Mother."

"I know, dear. What's done is done. But how are you in the First Circle right now?"

"Lucifer is making me traverse the 9 Circles before he'll discuss the release of a young man I know."

"You're planning to challenge the Prince of Darkness? Szymon, have you been doing drugs?"

"I have not been doing drugs, Mother. Well, I did take the blue pill--"

"Oh, I love the blue pill."

"Mother, I didn't know I had to fight him to the death, and if that's what I have to do then so be it. I don't half-ass anything. Even rescuing a gentleman in distress."

"Don't worry, Szymon. If it's possible for you to defeat him, you will. You've always had a surplus of perseverance and determination."

"Thank you, Mother. I love you. Take care of yourself."

"You take care of yourself. Keep an eye on him for me, Kurt."

"Will do, Mrs. Symanski."

Szymon bent down to give Sandy Szymanski a long hug. Kurt grinned and said, "Well, if this isn't nice, I don't know what is."

"One last thing, Szymon," said Sandy Symanski. "What year did you die?"

"2023. Why?"

"Did they cure the Corona Virus?"

"Yes, Mother. The vaccine is mostly effective. The pandemic is over."

"That's good. I should have gotten the vaccine."

"Goodbye, Mother."

Kurt led Szymon towards the Second Circle, weaving in and out between "people." Szymon noticed that there were several species of sentient beings among the residents of the First Circle. Among them were large rodents, standing upright and wearing clothes, and a female humanoid with purple skin and blue hair. He wished he had time to get to know them. They couldn't all be as bad as the green cube. As he thought of the Nixmarian, they appeared (or at least it was a member of their species) floating right toward them. Szymon hoped it was the latter.

"Apeman. I want you to take me with you."

"Why would I ever do that? I don't much care for you."

"I don't much care for you, but I admire your spirit. I believe you will complete your journey. That's why I would like to join you. I must get my revenge."

"I don't know. What do you think, Kurt? Do we need a snarky, green cube in our party?"

"Nixmarians are formidable allies. I don't see how it would hurt."

"Then it is settled. But no funny business."

"But what is funny about business?" asked the Nixmarian.

"Exactly. By the way, what is your name?"

"My name is Sherghim, second heir to the throne of Jarem."

"Ok, Sherg. Can I call you Sherg?"

"Please do not."

"Ok, Sherg. Good talk."

Chapter 6: Lust

"So, Kurt, how do we get down to the Second Circle? Is there an elevator?"

"Not exactly. You sure you don't want to stay for lunch? They're serving tofurkey and asparagus today. They only have Diet Pibb to drink, but you get used to it."

"No thanks. We shouldn't adventure on a full stomach, in case we have to do some swimming."

"If you insist. Well, you see that corridor? That is where we need to go."

Szymon saw a large cave opening in the side of the main cavern. It was only about a hundred yards away. They had been walking straight towards it.

"Oh, I see."

Once inside the corridor, they could see a short line of people that had formed in front of a circular chasm. On the edge of the chasm stood what appeared to be a naked, gray reptile man with a dark brown beard and a tall, gold crown on his head. He was several times the size of a human, and his serpent tail was long enough to coil it around himself nine times.

"That's the demon Minos, once the king of Crete," said Kurt. Let's skip this line; I know Minos personally."

As they approached the demon, the human at

the front of the line confessed his sins. When he was finished, Minos coiled his tail around himself six times.

"Six?" exclaimed the sinner. "I'm going to the Sixth Circle?"

Silently, Minos uncoiled his tail and wrapped the end of it around the sinner before lowering him into the chasm.

Not quite to the foot of Minos, Kurt gestured for Szymon and Sherghim to stay put as he convened with the demon.

After approaching, Kurt said, "Excuse me, Minos. Sorry for interrupting, but they're with me. Official business."

Minos nodded.

"How are you doing today?" asked Kurt.

"Another day in paradise. Living the dream. Another day, another dollar."

Kurt chuckled and replied, "At least you and I have jobs to keep us busy. The rest of Limbo spends eternity watching television."

"You are correct, but I would love to watch a little television. You know I don't even get breaks. I have to relieve myself down this hole. Which one is challenging Lucifer? The Human or the Nixmarian?"

"Oh, you've heard about that? It's the Human."

"Hell is a small place. Hmm, big odds against a human winning. I should place a bet. So where am I putting you?"

"Second Circle please."

Minos laid his tail flat and straight on the black cave floor, gesturing for them to get on. Kurt and Szymon climbed onto the tail.

Sherghim said "Last one there is a rotten goose," and descended into the chasm in a hurry.

Szymon thought, "Did they just say 'rotten goose?' Must be a bad translation." Shaking his head, he thought, "Oh well."

As the enormous, scaly, gray tail lowered Szymon and Kurt into the chasm, they noticed multiple winds that quickly grew in magnitude as they went down into the Second Circle. Scattered around them were many upon many wind-trapped sinners as far as the eye could see in all directions.   A good distance below them were people standing on the ground, being pushed in random directions and having trouble remaining standing.

The strong winds were coming from every direction and Kurt and Szymon had so much difficulty keeping their footing on the gray tail that they were both blown off and sent adrift within the hurricane-like conditions before Minos' tail retracted, leaving the 2nd Circle. Kurt and Szymon passed Sherghim, who was being buffeted in a circular pattern, and Sherghim asked them, "How am I supposed to get to the ground?"

Before the two could answer, one of the winds had blown them far away from the Nixmarian.

"Welcome to the Circle of Lust," shouted Kurt over the sounds of the winds. "Look, Szymon, it's Queen Victoria."

The winds then blew Kurt and Szymon in separate directions. With white hair and a high forehead, wearing the finest black dress, Queen Victoria flew by Szymon with a very unhappy look on her face. Szymon imagined her riding an old-fashioned bicycle past a flying farm house and chuckled before humming the witch theme from Wizard of Oz in his head. Next, he thought, "And this is the weakest punishment in Hell? An eternity of this would be agonizing. How do we get down from here?"

Still watching Queen Victoria, Szymon saw a stout, mostly-bald man with a white beard and gray mustache, wearing an oversized suit, fly toward Victoria with his arms outstretched as though he wanted to lock arms with the queen. Perhaps he wished to speak with her. When he got close, Victoria raised her leg and kicked out, pushing the man's large belly with her shoeless foot. He got caught in another wind and flew away.

When Szymon got close to Kurt again, he asked, "Who is the big guy in the suit?"

"That's Victoria's son, King Edward VII."

"That's Dirty Bertie? I guess his mom really doesn't care for him, does she?"

Before Kurt could answer, a partially-upward wind quickly pushed Szymon away from him, past a blonde-haired woman wearing black lingerie that was both sheer and translucent. Szymon immediately recognized her as Marylin Monroe. He noticed that she was less attractive when in distress, even in person, and he wondered why that mattered and why he even thought such a thing.

"I loved you in 'Some Like it Hot,'"blurted Szymon.

Marylin ignored Szymon, and he thought, "I probably shouldn't bother her. I can't even imagine how she feels after experiencing this for as long as she has."

That's when one of the winds pushed Szymon's top half backwards and another pushed his bottom half forward and he flipped upside down. Looking straight ahead, he saw Hugh Hefner, who was facing him nearby and was wearing a burgundy smoking jacket and black swim-shorts, and yelled, "Hey, Hef. I see you're also upside down."

"You get used to it after awhile. You should also get used to being in control of nothing but your daydreams, your bladder, and your bowels."

"You're funny. I always knew you would be funny in person."

Hugh was blown backwards quite a ways and Szymon faintly heard him yell, "It's an honor to meet a fan."

Szymon thought, "Does he think I read Playboy? Do I look like I read Playboy?"

Szymon looked down and decided he was at least a little closer to the ground, which was still a ways away. He faced his head forward again and saw Sherghim rapidly coming towards him.

"You any closer to figuring out a way to get to the ground?"

"No, Szymon. You?"

"That's a negative, Sherg. I'll keep trying."

Drifting backwards, Szymon bumped into someone and yelled, "Sorry," as he bounced off, spinning around about 180 degrees. Still upside-down, he saw a huge, jet-black humanoid with flesh of stone, wearing a thick, red tunic made of a felt-like fabric. The being growled, "Watch it, bub."

"Sorry."

After floating backwards a ways, opposing winds struck Szymon again. This time they pushed his sides, and he flipped right side up again. After doing so, the winds spun him around, and he saw an incredibly miserable, black and white cow fly past in the opposite direction. Szymon couldn't help but laugh. Then he was pushed towards Queen Victoria again.

"What do you have against Edward, your majesty?"

"Not that it's any of your business, but he reminds me too much of myself."

"You think that's why you both ended up in the same circle of Hell?"

"Are you calling us whores?"

"No, I'll leave that to God, the devil, and the historians, your majesty."

"Oh, you bite like a serpent, strangely clad man."

As Victoria spoke, Szymon spotted someone he hadn't seen in 50 years. He was headed straight towards him and, as he passed Queen Victoria, he told her, "By the way, women in the Western World have nearly equal rights to men now, no thanks to you, you self-degrading, old bat."

Victoria gasped and the man Szymon approached showed recognition of Szymon's identity.

"Szymon!" yelled the pale yet beautiful, 20-something year-old, with long black hair, wearing a hospital gown.

"Trevor! It's been 50 years, sweetheart. When did you die?"

"It was 1985, Szymon. I've missed you so much. I still love you."

Szymon's mind slipped down the rabbit hole again. He was 15. So was Trevor. The year was 1973. The two boys were alone in Szymon's bedroom, which was small and reeked of incense and marijuana. The walls were painted white and were mostly covered with rock and roll posters. Among the bands displayed were Pink Floyd, Led Zeppelin, The Doors, Janis Joplin, Jimi Hendrix, The Beatles, and the Grateful Dead.

The furniture was all wooden and included a chest of drawers with two lit, red candles on top, a desk with a clay lamp, a type-writer, and a lava lamp on it, a bed-side table with a record player (playing The White Album disc 1) sitting on top and with a milk crate full of records tucked beneath, and a bookshelf containing action figures (including Evel Knievel and the Lone Ranger), family photos, and a number of books.

Among the books were Doors of Perception, Siddhartha, 1984, Animal Farm, Fear & Loathing in Las Vegas, Fear & Loathing on the Campaign Trail, Jonathon Livingston Seagull, Dune, Dune Messiah, Stranger in a Strange Land, Sirens of Titan, and the entire J.R.R. Tolkein collection.

Two small piles of clothing lied on the floor in the middle of the room. Both boys were under the covers on Szymon's bed, wearing only their tight, white underwear. They were facing each other on their sides and Trevor kissed Szymon on the mouth before saying, "I'm ready, Szymon. Are you ready?"

"Ready for what?"

"To take our underwear off. Kissing is fun and all, but I want to do more." He stared into Szymon's eyes and awaited a response.

Frowning sadly, Szymon replied, "I'm not ready, Trevor. I'm sorry. Please don't be mad."

"Mad? I'm not mad. I didn't mean to make you feel bad. I just love you so much I want to take things to the next level. I'm tired of just kissing in our underwear every day. How about this. I won't ask again. I'll just wait until you tell me you're ready. You can take your time. All the time you need."

"Thank you, Trevor. I love you too."

Szymon kissed Trevor and grabbed his butt cheek with one hand.

"What the fuck!" yelled Szymon's father as he abruptly swung the bedroom door open. "Damn it, Trevor. I knew you were a faggot, you little trailer-trash motherfucker--I mean fatherfucker. Now get the fuck out of my house!"

Trevor jumped out of bed and started to put a leg in his pants when Szymon Sr. yelled, "Now! Pick up your clothes and run out of this house before I break your fucking face."

Trevor filled his arms with his clothes and ran down the stairs and out the front door. When Trevor left the bedroom, Szymon Sr. began taking off his belt.

"Get out of bed, Szymon. I'm gonna make you

wish you never met that boy."

Shaking like a paint mixer, his heartbeat racing, Szymon climbed out of his bed and bent over it with his teeth clenched and his white-knuckled, closed fists on the bed, ready to hold him in place.

Smack!

"One."

Smack!

"Two."

Smack!

"Three."

Smack!

"Four."

Smack!

"Five."

Smack!

"Six."

"Szymon, why is our son in his underwear?" asked Sandy Szymanski, standing in the doorway.

"I caught him kissing that Trevor boy in his bed. They were both in their goddamn underwear."

"So they were experimenting? Ok...Junior, do

you think you are a homosexual?"

"I don't know," answered Szymon with tears streaming down his face."

Szymon Sr. began weaving his belt back in place and said, "Well, no son of mine is going to be a goddamn butt-pirate. You know where you're going, Junior?"

"Hell?"

"Military school. They'll beat the gay out of you. Make you into a real man. The kind of man I can call my son."

Sandy interjected, "Honey, I think you're getting carried away."

"Nobody told you to think, woman. You're the one who thought buying him action figures wouldn't turn him into a faggot."

"I'm serious, Szymon. We don't need to be so drastic."

Szymon Sr. smacked the shit out of Sandy, knocking her on the floor.

"I'll teach you to talk back to me, bitch."

Szymon stood up straight and stepped between his mother and father, saying, "I won't let you hurt her anymore."

Szymon Sr. punched his son in the face with all

the strength in his right arm and said, "So now you want to be a man?"

Szymon immediately held his nose, which was broken and gushing blood.

"Well, it's too late, sissy boy. You'll be doing push-ups and respecting authority next week. You just wait."

Szymon came back to reality and saw that Trevor was getting close. He said, "I love you too, Trevor." As the two sinners neared each other, they placed their arms out to the front and locked arms with their hands on each other's forearms.

Trevor asked, "When did you die, Szymon?"

"I think it was today still."

"Really? Why are you wearing a white kimono?"

"Well, I performed Japanese ritual suicide so I could approach Lucifer about releasing a gay man I know."

"What the fuck?" Trevor said, inspecting Szymon's face with eyes wide as an owl's, detecting nothing but gravitas. "You're serious."

"I am. How did you die, Trevor?"

"I died of AIDS, Szymon. After you went off to military school, I was empty-hearted, and I became the school slut to fill the void you left. I let all the boys do what they wanted to me. And a teacher. I went to your house on Christmas in '75', looking for you. Your mom said you weren't there. Then your dad saw me and threatened to kill me if I ever showed my face again. I was nothing without you, Szymon. Then, after graduation, I moved to San Francisco to be a stripper. In the next 5 years, I had hundreds of sexual partners. Then I learned that I had HIV when I was 23. I developed AIDS when I was 25, and then I spent the next 2 years in the hospital with various illnesses, and died of pneumonia when I was only 27."

Chapter 7: Gluttony

When Szymon awoke, he was lying face up across the backs of a few sinners who were on their hands and knees in 2-3 feet of mud mixed with snow, piss, shit, and the vomit of the sinners as well as that of the demon Cerberus. Snow was gently landing on Szymon's face and melting when Szymon mumbled, "You don't go to Hell for being gay. You go here for being a slut (if you are one)." Kurt and Sherghim were standing/floating over him when Kurt spoke.

"You fainted, Szymon. We found you bouncing off people like a rag doll in a clothes dryer."

"How'd we get down from those winds?"

"Sherghim used their telekinesis to pull us down."

"Can you use that on yourself, Sherg?"

"No. Kurt threw me toward the ground and then I strategically bounced off people until I made it all the way down. It took some maneuvering."

"I bet. So this is the 3rd Circle?"

"Yep. Welcome to Gluttony, Szymon," answered Kurt.

"Smells like literal shit."

"It is. Are you ok to stand up, Szymon?"

Szymon replied, "Yes," and got to his feet. "Oh

God this is cold. And it's gonna leave one Hell of a stain."

He spoke the last words just before a giant, red worm with 3 heads slithered over from out of nowhere, through the countless sinners, much quicker than you would expect a worm to slither. The worm demon was roughly 10 feet tall and 30 feet long, with small mouths instead of eyes, and with normal-size snakes growing from its sides and wriggling all about.

The demon opened all 3 main mouths, its vomit-decayed teeth gnashing, and projectile-vomited on the 3 sinners. The vomit contained human bones and was greenish brown, smelling no different really than the infinite puddle of mud.

"Cerberus wants us to kneel down," said Kurt.

"Fuck. This is disgusting," said Szymon, looking down at the demon puke on his kimono.

The two humans kneeled and placed their hands on the ground beneath the layer of icy, cold mud. Sherghim lowered himself to inches above the mud, hoping to appease the beast.

"How do we get out of here," asked Szymon, choking on the odor and the taste of the air.

"Dante said he and Virgil got out by stuffing Cerberus' mouths full of mud and escaping down the chasm, which I believe is that way." Kurt used his head to point in the appropriate direction with an upwards nod.

"Ok. Worth a try."

Szymon grabbed a handful of mud and lunged toward Cerberus, who was still guarding them. The giant, 3-headed worm wasted no time evading Szymon's advance, zipping a great distance away in less than a second and then panting (as though smiling) with all 3 heads, its three massive tongues nearly touching the mud on the ground. You know how panting dogs look like they're smiling? Same thing, except it was a 3-headed worm. With teeth.

"It seems to be prepared this time," stated Sherghim.

"That's a shame," added Kurt.

As Szymon crawled the few feet back to his companions, he saw a face from his History books growing up. The 12th President of the United States, Zachary Taylor, saw Szymon look at him and said, "You. In the dress. Fetch me some fresh cherries. I like them with iced milk. You can manage that, yes?"

"Yes, iced milk. In Hell. I'll get right on that." answered Szymon before thinking, "What a fucking moron."

"So whadaya think, Kurt?" Szymon asked when he returned to him and Sherghim.

"We should head toward the chasm and see what the situation is."

"Sounds good."

The 3 adventurers crawled/floated in the suspected direction of the chasm. As they did so, they passed some of the most unhappy faces they had ever laid eyes on.

"Well, I'll be damned," exclaimed Kurt. "It's King Henry I of England."

Henry heard his name and asked, "Who knows my name?"

"Me. Kurt Vonnegut of America."

"America. I've heard of this place. Is it true they have horseless carriages?"

"And hollow birds made of swords," interrupted Szymon, "that take people to Disneyland."

"Disney? Is he French? I hate the French."

"No," answered Kurt."

"He's worse than French," added Szymon. "He's a neo-nazi."

Kurt stifled laughter and asked, "So, your majesty, how was the barrel of lampreys that did you in?"

"Oh, I'll be happy if I never see another lamprey for as long as I live."

Sherghim interjected. "That can be arranged, Earth man."

"Is that a talking flan?" asked King Henry. "Be
70

you wizards?"

"Yes, we be wizards, your majesty," answered Szymon. "So, have you seen a large hole around here? We're going to use it to get back to Kansas."

"There is a circular wall not far from here. That direction." King Henry nodded toward the wall. "Perhaps it is a well."

"Thank you, your majesty," replied Kurt. "Come on, fellas."

The 3 continued forward, still fighting every urge to vomit.

"Well, he was nice enough," said Szymon.

"He sentenced his older brother to life in prison for trying to steal his throne."

"Sounds fair," replied Sherghim. "Death would have been too merciful."

"Finally, Sherg. We agree on something."

"Don't get used to it, ape man."

"You 2 be nice. Don't make me pull this thing over."

Kurt and Szymon both laughed and Sherghim replied, "I don't get it."

Following a few moments of silence, Szymon recognized a Japanese man wearing a midnight-blue kimono with   a pattern of gold diamond-clusters on it.

"Master Akihiro!"

The large-built, elderly man showed recognition as his wet eyes brightened and opened wide. That was when Szymon's mind slipped down the rabbit hole yet again.

The year was 1977. Szymon was 19 and was balancing on one foot, which was inside of a hand-crafted sandal and was holding up his body on top of a bamboo pole. He was facing Akihiro, who was standing on 2 bamboo poles. They both wore Japanese samurai fencing kimonos, or kendos (Szymon's white, Akihiro's black) and they both held katanas of excellent craftsmanship. Below them was a pond. The several tall, bamboo poles were buried a few feet deep in the pond floor.

"If you cannot stand on bamboo, you cannot stand on the winds, Szymon-san. Do you understand?"

"Yes, Sensei."

"Good. Now I want you to attack me."

"Yes, Sensei."

Szymon held his katana at his side with his right hand, the blade pointing downward, as he bent his right leg and jumped to another pole. He landed on the pole with his left foot and quickly lifted his sword as he placed his right foot on a nearby pole to keep his balance.

"The water is cold, Szymon-san."

"I know, Sensei."

Szymon looked at his target and saw that there were no poles near the 2 his sensei stood on. Szymon thought, "I must be a kamakazi. He will not be expecting that." Szymon jumped, pushing off with his left leg, his right arm and his sword pointing straight behind him, and stepped on a pole with his right foot, immediately pushing off, straight and low, lunging toward Akihiro. Szymon raised his sword with both hands, the blade pointing to the right till it was behind him, and swung it forward with full force, the blade arcing to the left.

Akihiro pushed the 2 poles he stood on outward with his sandaled feet, bending them so that he could do the splits, avoiding Szymon's attack entirely. Szymon flew above his master, eventually landing in the pond water. He immediately stood, the surface of the water at his neck, and shook his head, his long brown hair splattering water in the wind.

"Nice try, Szymon-san. I take it you thought you were a kamakazi pilot. Very brave. But bravery can be very stupid, Szymon-san."

"Yes, Sensei."

"Fetch the water for supper and meet me inside, Szymon-san."

"Yes, Sensei."

As Szymon pulled the rope that was lifting the bucket from the well, Akihiro's teenage daughter, Kotori, approached, moving her hips with extra force. She wore a red kimono decorated with gold cherry blossoms, with her hair up.

"Hello, Szymon-san. How was training?"

"I still can't defeat your father." Szymon pulled the bucket off the hook and set it on the ground.

"Neither can my father. I wouldn't let it bother you, Szymon-san."

"Thank you, Kotori."

"Don't mention it. I was cold, alone in my bed last night."

"So was I. That's what happens on cold nights, Kotori."

"Why won't you let me get close to you, Szymon-san?

"I've already told you. My tab A goes into slots C and D only. You have no Tab A. You are ill equipped, Kotori."

"You're no fun!"

"Sorry, Kotori. Are we having puffer fish again?

"Of course. You know my father is addicted."

"Eating puffer fish is brave. But bravery can be very stupid."

Kotori laughed her ass off and exclaimed, "That was a very good impression!"

"Thanks. I better bring in the water."

Szymon woke up to see Akihiro's woeful face with a couple decades worth of extra wrinkles decorating it.

"Szymon-san. What has brought you here? You were not a glutton when I knew you."

"I'm headed to the 9th Circle to challenge Lucifer."

"You are challenging the dark prince? I always knew you were brave. But bravery can be very stupid."

"Yes, I know, Sensei. But it is my destiny."

"Destiny is an excuse to be stupid, Szymon-san."

"Yes, I know, Sensei. Everything is stupid."

Akihiro raised his muddy hand and patted Szymon's shoulder.

Kurt said, "Sorry to interrupt, but we must continue our mission."

"Yes, Kurt. I'm sorry. Farewell, Sensei."

The party continued forward and Kurt asked, "Was that your karate teacher?"

"Yes. And swordsmanship. Akihiro was a great

ronin. A samurai of no comparison."

"He died from puffer fish poison. Did he tell you that?"

"He did? He did! Gluttony can be very stupid!" Szymon laughed.

Kurt patted Szymon on the back and said, "We can't save everyone, Szymon."

"Thanks, Kurt. You are a good friend. Can I call you my friend?"

"Of course you can, Szymon."

"How do you say it on Earth?" asked Sherghim. "Oh yeah...Get a room you two."

They all laughed boisterously. That's when Kurt noticed another historical figure in the distance.

"See the man in the black satin robe? With light brown hair? That's the Danish astronomer, Tycho Brahe, who believed the other planets revolved around the sun, but the sun revolved around the Earth, which didn't move at all."

"Oh, so he's a wacko," said Szymon.

"The Human ego never ceases to surprise me," added Sherghim.

Szymon replied, "Oh yeah. 'Cause he thought Earth was the center of the universe," and then asked Kurt, "How did he die?"

"He needed to urinate during an important banquet but didn't, so he could eat dessert. The autopsy showed he had urine in his blood."

"Holy Hell!"

"There are many ways for a genius to be an idiot, and vice versa."

"Indeed, Kurt. Indeed."

A woman nearby then puked, and another sinner puked because of the sound, and then another...Szymon and Kurt held back their own vomit and Szymon wondered, "Does Sherg puke? Do they even eat?"

Looking ahead of themselves, the travelers noticed a wall of dull black stones that apparently circled around the chasm leading to the 4th Circle.

"There it is!"

"Sherghim," Szymon said. "Can you scout ahead at a great height where Cerberus can't reach you, and may not even spot you?"

"On it."

Sherghim returned momentarily, saying, "It's the chasm, alright. And I saw one of those black and white Earth beasts eating mud next to the wall."

It took a second to add up to something in his head before Szymon thought, "Oh! A cow. I wonder if it's the same one from the 2nd Circle. Probably not."

"Did you see Cerberus?" Kurt asked Sherghim.

"No, I did not."

"Good. Fuck this shit! Let's run," exclaimed Szymon. He got up and began sprinting as fast as he was able to in deep mud. Kurt followed behind him. Sherghim went up a great height as he floated forward.

When they all got to the wall, Cerberus appeared, its tongues nearly dragging the mud.

"Shit," said Szymon. "It beat us here. How did it do that without eyes?" Szymon drew his sword from the invisible sheath, the blade glowing light blue. He charged toward Cerberus, his katana raised at the ready.

Before Szymon reached Cerberus, the great, red worm-demon slithered around the chasm close to the wall at an amazing speed and continued around it again and again, picking up speed until it was only a red blur. When Szymon reached the short wall surrounded by a tall red blur, he swung his sword but only bounced off the barrier created by Cerberus, landing on his back in the mud.

Szymon was winded for a moment, and then said, "This is impossible."

Cerberus continued circling the chasm and Szymon felt despair set in.

"We need some sort of diversion," said Kurt.

That was when President Zachary Taylor stood

up a distance behind them, saying, "I believe I can be of assistance."

"Holy shit," exclaimed Szymon. "You've been following us."

"I have," replied the president. "I knew you would need my assistance, and that you might be able to--"

"Get you some cherries and iced milk! What the fuck?" Then Szymon remembered the cow near the chasm. Then he remembered the trick Kurt had taught him. "Well, Mr. President, you ready to see how a true wizard gets past a giant worm-demon?"

"I am intrigued."

"As am I," added Kurt.

Szymon sheathed his katana and then, closing his eyes, reached into his kimono and pulled out his favorite large, green ceramic bowl. He then yelled at Sherghim, who was still far above the chasm. "Which way is that Earth beast?"

"To your left, Szymon."

Szymon walked around the red blur to the left and found the cow, which had no problem with him borrowing some milk. Szymon returned with the bowl of milk and handed it to Kurt. "Can you hold this for a minute?"

"Of course."

"I hope the cherries I left in the crisper bin of my fridge are still good. I don't know how time passes in Hell. It still feels like it's been only a day, but who knows?"

Szymon reached into his kimono and pulled out a bag of cherries. They were still fresh and Szymon grinned triumphantly.

"That IS magic!" said President Taylor. "I knew I could count on you."

"That's nice, Mr. Rough and Ready. Hey, Kurt. Is that milk collecting snow?"

"Not much."

"Damn. Well, I can't remember if I filled my ice tray the last time I used ice. Here's hoping."

Szymon pulled a white ice tray from his kimono that was full of ice.

"Hell yeah. Here, Kurt. Hold the cherries."

Szymon reached down, grabbed his Kimono in the front, and held it up so that there was a pocket or basket created by the cloth. He then dumped the ice into the recess and tossed the ice tray into the mud. Next, Szymon closed the cloth around the ice before punching it repeatedly. He poured the crushed ice into the bowl of milk Kurt was still holding when President Taylor spoke.

"I'll need 2 bowls actually."

"Why two?"

"One for the demon. One for me."

Szymon reached into his kimono to pull out another ceramic bowl, this one orange. He split the milk and ice into two portions and did the same with the cherries.

"Well, here you go, Mr. President."

President Taylor took the two bowls and said, "You boys should split up and walk to my right and left. Step over that wall as soon as the red blur vanishes."

"Thank you, Mr. President."

"Thank YOU, Mr. wizard."

Kurt and Szymon did as the president suggested, and ole Rough and Ready approached the red blur and soothingly said, "Here Cerberus. Here boy. You want some cherries and milk? I know you like sweets."

Cerberus came to an abrupt stop, panting harder than usual. President Taylor held out one of the large bowls and Cerberus swallowed it whole with his middle head as the 3 adventurers leapt/dropped into the chasm. The president said, "Well, he forgot to get me a spoon. Oh well." He put his face in the bowl of the same dessert that killed him 170 years earlier and ate.

Chapter 8: Greed

After a moment of falling down the chasm, Szymon and Kurt fell into a pond of the darkest water Szymon had ever seen. The pond was not deep enough to cushion the landing entirely, so the two humans swam out of the pond with aching legs. Sherghim had beat them to the shore.

A short distance ahead of the 3 sinners was a massive, elaborately-built golden gate allowing entrance through 2 towering gold walls. Ahead of the gate stood a tremendous, entirely-gold statue of a well-built young man wearing a toga and a symmetrical crown of 8 dragon horns. The statue was nearly as tall as the golden gate.

"That's a cool statue," said Szymon.

"That's Plutus, the guardian of Greed."

Once Kurt was finished speaking, the great statue asked, "Be you hoarders or wasters?"

Kurt answered, "We are neither."

"Then you do not belong here."

"Lucifer has sent for us. We must pass."

"You shall not pass."

"Listen here, Plutus, you evil, little brat," Kurt said loudly, with a surplus of contempt in his voice. "You think you can do as you wish, inciting avarice in the weak, making the poor poorer and the rich richer, inspiring people to hoard or waste instead of sharing and finding true fortune in the fellowship of others? Well, I'm over it. And your parents aren't here to protect you from my wrath. You let us through or I will stand here for eternity belittling you. It's up to you, Prince Avarice. Ha! God of Wealth. More like the God of being a spoiled prick. You're no better than Loki."

Silently, Plutus opened the gate and stepped aside, waiting and then closing it behind the adventurers. Inside the walls was a vast city of gold. Everything was made of gold, including the main street which the 3 traveled down.

Once they were out of earshot, Szymon exclaimed, "Kurt, that was mesmerizing. You are my new hero."

"Thank you. Tip jar's on the piano. Don't forget to tip your waitress."

Sherghim immediately asked, "Why do you speak in gibberish? I see no piano. There are no waitresses."

"It's a figure of speech," interjected Szymon.

"A what?"

"It's ok," Said Kurt. "I'll try to speak in plain English from now on, Sherghim."

The golden road had no sidewalks, for it was for foot traffic only. The street was lined with various shops. They were all upscale shops selling the most luxurious finery and other items and services that wouldn't be considered necessities. One shop only sold gold spoons that were made specifically for cracking soft-boiled eggs. It had a gold spoon-shaped sign outside that read, "Mr. Dumpty's."

"Who runs the shops? Imps?" asked Szymon.

"No," answered Kurt. "Greed is divided into 2 factions: the Hoarders and the Wasters. The Hoarders run the shops. The Wasters rob the shops and spend the loot at other shops."

"That's the dumbest thing I've ever heard."

"I agree with the ape man. That shit is dumb."

"Why do you only call me ape man? Kurt is Human as well."

"He does not resemble an ape."

"Oh, but I do?" replied Szymon.

At that moment, a young man wearing a tuxedo exited a tuxedo shop, pushing a gold wheelbarrow full of gold coins, and yelled inside the shop on his way out, "Why do you hoard?" An older man wearing a sweater and slacks and heavily-scuffed shoes exited soon after, yelling, "Give me back my gold!"

"Should we help him?" asked Szymon.

"That would be a waste of time. It's probably the 100th time he's been robbed today."

"Oh, well damn."

"Why do they fight over gold? Nixmar has plenty of gold. Must be an Earth thing."

"What do they fight over on Nixmar, Sherg?" asked Szymon.

"Fruit."

"Any particular fruit?" asked Kurt.

"Mostly farqennapels."

"Oh, yes. Farqennapels," mocked Szymon. "Can you describe them?"

"They're black. Taste like a gym sock. And very spicy. They only grow on volcanoes, so they're a rare commodity."

"Sounds delicious."

"Be nice, Szymon," said Kurt.

"You mock me?" asked Sherghim.

"You mock me?" mocked Szymon. "Wait a second. How do you know what a gym sock tastes like?"

"I've visited Earth before, ape man. Earth had the best gym socks I've ever eaten."

"You are a weird creature, Sherg."

As Szymon spoke, a dozen men and women

wearing fine clothing emerged from the alley ahead, to the right of the travelers, pushing gold wheelbarrows full of gold coins and various valuables. The Wasters were running as fast as they could with heavy loads, and turned right, onto the main street in front of Szymon and company. Behind the Wasters, a dozen people who were modestly dressed, with old shoes on their feet, chased after. The Hoarders yelled, "Why do you waste? Why do you waste?"

"Wow. This is like a bad dream. Or acid trip. Glad we're not stuck here forever."

Kurt nodded in agreement. "Reminds me of a Stanley Kubrick film."

"Which one?"

"All of them."

"So how do we get out of here?"

The Wasters with the freshly stolen wheelbarrows entered a golden casino that took up 4 square blocks and rose 21 stories, most of which consisted of hotel rooms. Over the entrance was a sign that read, "Walton Manor," in Roman letters.

Kurt answered, "Easy, Szymon. The unguarded chasm is at the other end of this road."

"So no hurricanes or worm dogs?"

"Nope."

"Excellent."

87

As they approached the casino, they neared a female fortune teller, who sat in front, on a folding chair, her crystal ball and tarot cards sitting on a card table with a violet tablecloth draped over it. It was mostly hidden by the tablecloth, but Szymon could see a gold wheelbarrow beneath the table. The woman smiled directly at Szymon.

"I know your fortune," stated the fortune teller.

"You do?" asked Szymon.

"Yes. You will win all the moneys. In the casino. At the Wheel of Fortune."

"Is that like roulette?"

"Yes."

"Ok, what number is the winner?"

"I need more information. What is your birthday, year, and time?

"January 27th, 1958 at um...2:37 a.m."

"Oh, Aquarius. What is your mother's maiden name?"

"Kowalczyk."

"Polish. What was your first pet's name?"

"Batman. He was the wealthiest Guinea pig in Gotham City. Didn't need superpowers because he had a trust fund."

"That's funny. What street did you grow up on?"

"Hey, wait a minute! I've heard of this. You're a computer hacker."

"It's ok, Szymon," interrupted Kurt. "You didn't own a computer or cell phone. Said so in your file. So she can't hack you...if you don't have passwords."

"Okay, fine. I lived on Poplar Street."

"Ah," said Kurt. "The suburbs. Where they chop down the trees and name roads after them."

The fortune teller looked into her crystal ball and said, "37. The winning number is 37."

"Thanks, madame. What do I owe you?"

"Nothing. It's on the house. Just remember me in the future."

"Will do."

Szymon turned to face Kurt and Sherghim, saying, " Can we go inside the casino for a moment? I have a plan."

"Sure, they have hors d'oeuvres. I'm famished."

When the 3 sinners entered the casino lobby, they saw the typical casino amenities, like rows of slot machines, craps tables, and blackjack tables, only they were made of gold. From the ceiling hung gold and diamond chandeliers. The men and women running the casino all appeared to be Hoarders, who were dressed nicely but not nearly as nicely as the Wasters. The Wasters that the 3 had followed into the casino were standing in line with their wheelbarrows, waiting to trade "their" gold in for casino chips.

Szymon immediately stepped in line and Kurt went in search of hors d'oeuvres.

"So, Sherg. You guys have casinos on Nixmar?"

"No."

"Do Nixmarians gamble?"

"You mean trade everything for nothing? We have ways of doing that."

"So you understand the concept."

"Yes."

"And you understand that gambling is addictive and that addiction is a disease."

"Yes. So why is it punished in Hell? Is it normal to punish people for being sick?"

"Unfortunately."

"The Universe is more repulsive than I ever knew, ape man."

"You're telling me, Sherg."

"So how do you plan to acquire plastic coins?"

"Like this."

Szymon reached into his kimono and pulled out a baseball card in a thick plastic sleeve with screws tightened in the corners. The card was blue and boasted a picture of Babe Ruth.

"A picture of a fat man?"

"A fat athlete. Earth's greatest athlete."

Kurt returned with a gold tray holding pigs in blankets.

"Ah, the 1914 Babe Ruth rookie card you stole from the ruler of Abu Dhabi."

"One and the same."

Szymon reached the bank window as the last Waster in line ahead of him walked off with his wheelbarrow full of chips.

"What can I do for you?" asked the woman behind the bullet-proof glass window.

"I want to trade this for chips," answered Szymon.

"Ah, a Babe Ruth rookie card. Let me speak to my boss."

The woman picked up the receiver of a golden telephone and dialed a number. Szymon could barely hear the conversation, so he turned to Kurt.

"So, Kurt. You glad we waited to eat?" He

grabbed a pig in a blanket off the tray and shoved it into his mouth. "This is way better than tofurkey."

"Yes, I agree, Szymon."

One of the pigs in a blanket raised off the tray on its own and flew quickly toward Sherghim, entering the gelatinous cube and resting in the center of Sherghim's body.

"So, that's how you eat."

"Sir?" the banker interrupted politely.

"Yes?"

"The owner said we can give you 2 million in chips."

"That will work." Szymon handed the woman the card.

"Ok, your chips are behind the 1st door. May you be blessed by fortune."

"Thanks."

Szymon found his wheelbarrow full of chips and led the party of adventurers toward the Wheel of Fortune. There were Wasters with wheelbarrows standing around every gambling table. Whenever a Waster lost a bet, he or she yelled, "Why do you hoard?" at the dealer taking their money. As Szymon, Kurt, and Sherghim neared the Wheel of Fortune, they saw that the croupier at the large golden wheel mounted to the wall was none other than Thomas

Edison.

"Is that?"

"Thomas Edison. In the flesh."

"Oh, I hate that guy," said Szymon.

"I take it you know about him ripping off Nikolai Tesla?"

"Among countless other inventors."

"Did you know he electrocuted an elephant to death with Tesla's A/C electricity to prove it was dangerous?" asked Kurt.

"I've seen the black and white footage. Poor Topsy. Deserved better than to get mixed up with such a psychopath."

"I concur."

When they arrived at the wheel, Edison said, "You do not look like wasters."

"You do not look like an elephant-murdering thief."

"Ooh, you have a mouth on you. I cannot wait to take your money."

"Too bad, Edison. I'm going to win."

"Nobody ever wins at the Wheel of Fortune."

"Well, there's always a first time for everything,

motherfucker."

"Place your bet then."

"I bet it all on 37."

"Ha! There is no 37, genius. The wheel goes to 36."

"Fuck!" thought Szymon. "The gypsy lied to me. I can't believe I trusted her."

Noticing the panic on Szymon's face, Kurt whispered, "It's ok, Szymon. Counting the zero, there are 37 numbers on the wheel."

"36 is the 37th number! Thanks Kurt. Thomas, I bet it all (2 million) on 36."

"Very well."

With both his white-gloved hands, Edison spun the wheel hard and fast. The wheel spun round and round and round. And round. Finally, it slowed down and Szymon saw 36 coming around toward the arrow at the top just fast enough to make it to it's target. He held his breath as the pin next to the 36 panel pushed on the arrow before the wheel stopped entirely.

Szymon screamed in excitement, jumping up and down. Thomas Edison looked flabbergasted. Kurt shook Szymon's hand and said, "Congratulations, Szymon. What will you do with the money?"

"I'm going to Disneyland," said Szymon, short of breath."

Thomas Edison wrote Szymon a claims ticket for 70 million dollars and slapped it into Szymon's hand as unpleasantly as possible.

"You like apples, Thomas?"

Edison looked perplexed.

"How 'bout...you shove some apples up your ass, Thomas?"

Szymon spun around dramatically and strutted toward the bank window with Kurt and Sherghim following closely behind. When Szymon got to the window, the banker woman said, "What can I do for you?"

"I'd like to talk to the owner. About purchasing this fine establishment."

"Oh!" said the banker. "I will give him a call. Please wait here while I talk to him."

Szymon looked at Kurt, who was dying to speak.

"You're buying the casino? What for? We're leaving this circle for good."

"You'll see, Kurt. You'll see."

"Sir?" interrupted the banker. "Mr. Walton will see you now. You will find his office on the 21st floor."

The elevator was located nearby and, when the 3 sinners reached it, Szymon said, "I need you 2 to wait downstairs. I wish to negotiate this purchase on my own."

"I'm not supposed to let you out of my sight, Szymon."

"Oh, Kurt. After all we've been through together, you still don't trust me?"

"Oh, I trust you. But Sam Walton? I don't trust the founder of Wal-Mart as far as I can throw him."

"Is that who runs this place?"

"It's called Walton Manor, Szymon."

"Oh yeah. Well, don't worry. I've done business with scarier men."

"Ok, Szymon. We'll be outside. I want to get a Tarot reading."

"Ok. Good luck."

"Same to you."

When Szymon entered the elevator, the operator asked what floor.

"21st floor."

"You're the one who won 70 million? Can I see your claims ticket?"

Szymon showed it to the man, who nodded, inserted a key into the control panel, punched a code into a keypad, and pressed the button that said "21."

The man was silent the entire way to the 21st floor. When the elevator stopped and the door slid open, Szymon saw a foyer entirely made of gold and an open entrance leading to an office made of gold.

"Szymon, please join me in my office."

As szymon stepped through the doorway, he drew his katana, the blue aura glowing bright. He heard a cough and swung the sword to the left and then to the right. Both the men Szymon had sliced in half collapsed, their severed bodies falling to the floor with a total of 4 loud thuds.

"How did you know?"

"How does a goose know to fly South?"

"I am Sam Walton."

"I know who you are."

"Good. And you are?"

"Szymon Szymanski. I'm the contender to Lucifer's throne."

"Ah. I wish I had known that before I tried to rob you."

"I bet you do. Let me make this simple, Sam. I'm going to give you the 70 million. But I want the deed for the Casino, and I want you to place a bet for me."

"What am I betting on?"

"The death match. You're gonna bet 35 million on me to win."

"Sounds fair. Why do you trust me to place a bet?"

"Oh, I think you know better than to fuck with me again."

"Fair enough."

As, Szymon and Sam hammered out the details, Kurt got his Tarot read outside the casino.

"Ooh, your last card is The Hanged Man. This means you need to let go of old patterns and welcome a metamorphosis."

"Wow. It means all that? What old patterns?"

"Probably working for Lucifer."

"Oh. Yeah. What metamorphosis?"

"The upcoming shift in power in Hell."

"Oh! So Lucifer dies?"

"I didn't say that."

"How much do I owe you?"

"Oh no. If you're with the contender, it's free of charge."

"Contender?"

"To the throne."

"Oh. Gee, everyone seems to know about that."

"I know all things, Mr. Vonnegut."

Kurt laughed, and his laughter was cut off by loud shrieks and screams from inside the casino.

"Szymon."

The front doors swung open and Szymon exited, holding his katana in one hand and Thomas Edison's head in the other, gripping it by the hair. He sheathed his sword and handed the fortune teller the deed to the casino.

"Told you I'd remember you. You're going to need to hire new guards though. The old ones were terminated."

"Thank you, Contender."

"I leave you alone for 1 minute," said Kurt. "So how much did he charge you?"

"I gave him 35 million."

"And the rest of the winnings?"

"I bet the rest on me to defeat Lucifer."

"So that's your plan!"

"You like it?"

99

"I do. You ready to leave?"

"Yeah, let's blow this popsicle stand. Oh, sorry Sherg. Let's get out of Dodge. I mean, time to leave."

"Yes, it's time to leave," agreed Sherghim.

When they got to the edge of town, they saw the chasm toward the 5th Circle across a dark brown river.

"Oh shit. We better wait 20 minutes, Kurt."

"What?" blurted Sherghim. "Wait for what?"

"Humans can't swim for 20 minutes after eating."

"That is absurd."

"It's true."

"Then allow me to give you a lift."

Sherghim lifted both humans with their mind and the 3 floated across the river. Talk about multi-tasking.

Chapter 9: Anger

The three adventurers descended the chasm at a moderate speed as Sherghim used their telekinesis to move Szymon and Kurt down the chasm alongside them. The chasm opened up and there was a deep, filthy swamp that was covered by a thick fog and that went on forever. Sherghim stopped in their tracks, stopping the 2 humans' descents a distance above the water.

"Thank God for alien magic powers," said Szymon. "I don't need a cramp right now. So now what, Kurt?"

"Welcome to the Circle of Anger," said Kurt, who then asked, "Sherghim, can you move us near that ship?" He pointed at a pirate ship not too far off.

The ship's prow boasted a figurehead of a snarling Siberian Husky carved from a dark wood. The ship itself was large for a pirate ship, and was quite an impressive vessel, constructed from lighter-colored wood than the figurehead. As the floating sinners neared the ship, they passed over several miserable people drowning in the swamp, including a red-headed man with one ear.

"Vincent Van Gogh. Poor guy doesn't deserve this punishment."

"What's he here for, Kurt? Being depressed?"

"Basically."

"That's fucked."

As the travelers approached the ship, floating through the air, a bearded, long-haired Russian man holding an iron staff, with a fur-rimmed crown on his head, walked to the bow's edge and said, "Be you nobles or serfs?"

"We are serfs," answered Kurt.

"Good. You have permission to board."

"Is that Ivan the Terrible?"

"Sure is, Szymon. He should be a valuable ally."

Sherghim rested Kurt and Szymon on the ship's deck and Ivan said, "I am Ivan Vasilyevich, Tzar of Russia. Who are you?"

There were a number of people aboard the ship and most of them were on the deck, working. Some were manning the sails, 2 were swabbing the deck with dirty mops.

"It's an honor, Tzar Ivan. I am Kurt Vonnegut, social satirist of America."

"I am Szymon Symanski, contender to Lucifer's throne."

"I am Sherghim, 2nd heir to the throne of Nixmar."

"Ah, but you said you were serfs."

Kurt replied, "They are noble by title, but a serf

102

in spirit."

"How do you feel about the redistribution of wealth?" Ivan asked Sherghim.

"I do not believe in wealth," answered Sherghim. "Let them eat fruit."

"Be you a wizard?"

"All members of my species possess these powers."

"Very interesting. I would be honored to have you all fight by my side."

"Who are we fighting?" asked Kurt.

"Queen Mary. I loathe her very existence."

"Bloody Mary?" asked Szymon.

"She'll be bloody when I'm finished with her," answered Ivan.

"Ha! Fuck Bloody Mary. She burned alive so many Protestants. You need me to do anything, Tzar Ivan?" asked Szymon.

"All you need to do is equip a weapon and prepare to be boarded."

Szymon drew his katana, the aura glowing a soft blue.

"Done and done."

103

"What a magnificent weapon."

"It's made from my life force."

"I don't have a weapon," said Kurt.

"Then go down and help load the cannons."

"Aye aye, Captain."

Kurt left and Sherghim said, "Tzar Ivan. What did the nobles do to make you so bitter towards them?"

"They performed every form of treachery attempting to take my throne. Or drive me mad. They even poisoned my beloved wife," Ivan said, fuming, his voice gaining animosity towards the end.

"Doesn't sound much different than Nixmar. The nobility can be an underhanded lot. That is certain."

At that moment, another ship became visible through the fog. It was smaller than Ivan's and had a figurehead of a spaniel dog.

"Mary and the Sacred Spaniel!" exclaimed Ivan as he signaled for the helmsman to turn the ship to the right. "Ready the cannons!"

The approaching vessel turned left to face side by side with the Hungry Husky. When they were completely parallel, Ivan shouted, "Fire!"

Both ships exchanged cannon fire. The Hungry

Husky was hit by 3 cannonballs and was shaken briefly but violently. That was when several people wearing clothing from different time periods and different geological locations swung from ropes and boarded Ivan's ship. A man holding a pirate cutlass and wearing a white toga landed on the deck in front of Szymon.

"I will feed you to the lions," yelled the bald man with hairy shoulders.

"I AM a lion, asshole," replied Szymon as he met the man with swords crossed. They blocked each other's blows several times before Szymon stomped on the man's sandaled foot with his own bare foot. The man dropped his sword, which fell and pierced his other foot. He screamed as Szymon immediately swung his katana, beheading the man entirely.

Szymon looked to his left to see Ivan handling himself against a man wearing only black socks, brown underwear, and a 20th century U.S. drill instructor's hat. Szymon recognized the man immediately and slipped down the rabbit hole.

The year was 1975. Szymon was 17 and was wearing military fatigues minus the blouse and hat, with his head shaved. He was running toward a tall wooden wall with two long hanging ropes that were resting against the face of the wall and were spaced out from each other to accommodate 2 soldiers. Szymon jumped to grip one of the ropes with both hands, straddling the rope with his boot-heels pushing on the wall. Halfway up the wall, Szymon lost his grip with one of his hands, and his feet slipped. He hung by

105

one hand for a moment, struggling to regain his grip and his footing before losing hold of the rope and falling to the ground.

"Symanski! What is your malfunction, you pudgy, little shit? A chain is only as strong as its weakest link," yelled the drill instructor standing near the wall with an olive campaign hat on his head, a stop-watch in his hand, and a whistle hanging from his neck. "You can't get your ass over my wall? Then get your ass over here, Symanski."

Szymon ran to the drill instructor and snapped to attention.

"Symanski. Go ahead and go to chow. Then meet me in my quarters."

"Yes Sir."

After chow, Szymon slunk through the halls toward Sergeant Anderson's quarters. The hallway was lit, and the windows revealed nightfall, the sun having said farewell for the night.

"I need to put a stop to this," thought Szymon. "But what do I do?"

Reaching the drill sergeant's quarters, Szymon took a deep breath, frowning like a depressed widow.

"Come in, Szymanski. And close the door."

Szymon entered, closing the door behind him. He stood there, boiling with rage and staring into nothingness. Sitting on the edge of his bed in his

106

underwear, his green hat on his head, Sergeant Anderson spoke impatiently.

"What are you waiting for, Symanski? Undress. I am a busy man."

"No, I'm not doing it this time."

"What the fuck do you mean, cadet? We have a deal. I let you graduate next month and I never tell your dad you're still a fag. And you let me get that sweet, fat ass."

"No more ass, shit-head."

"Fuck you, Symanski, you little shit. You attacked me and I shot you in self-defense."

Sergeant Anderson quickly opened the drawer on his nightstand and reached for his M-1911 .45 caliber pistol but it wasn't there. Szymon raised his right arm, holding the missing pistol in his hand.

"But how?"

"Magic, motherfucker."

Szymon pulled the trigger and Sergeant Anderson's head erupted in blood and brain matter. Szymon heard quick footsteps and turned to see another cadet open the door.

"Szymon, what have you done?"

"What had to be done. He was a monster."

"Well, you better run. They'll hang you for

this."

Still gripping the pistol, Szymon ran down the hall.

That was when Szymon's mind snapped awake, and he immediately watched Ivan the Terrible get stabbed through the heart with Sergeant Anderson's cutlass.

"No!" Szymon rushed up to where the Tzar had collapsed on the ground and stopped, staring blankly at Sergeant Anderson. The ships exchanged cannon fire again, the Hungry Husky and everyone aboard shaking briefly.

"Symanski! I finally get my revenge."

"You wish!"

Szymon reached into his kimono and pulled out the .45 caliber he had kept as a memento of his first kill.

"How do you have that gun?"

"Magic, motherfucker."

Szymon pulled the trigger again and again until the gun was out of rounds, the bullets sending Sergeant Anderson over the edge of the ship. Szymon was breathing heavily and he turned around, looking for Sherghim. He found them, where they were using their mind to throw a Zulu woman off the ship into the swamp. The woman wore only a grass skirt, her breasts hanging from her chest, and she growled as her body was flung into the water.

Members of Ivan's crew had dispatched the other attackers except for 1. Szymon approached the last attacker: a viking wearing armor and a helmet with mounted bull horns.

"Allow me," said Sherghim, who used their mind to lift the viking and slam him down onto the ship's deck. The viking dropped his sword, and Sherghim slammed him into the deck twice more before tossing him overboard.

"Thank you, Sherg."

"Don't mention it."

From the bow of the Sacred Spaniel where she stood, Mary yelled, "Death to the Russian Orthodox Church!"

Bloody Mary's ship then retreated. Szymon approached Ivan and knelt down beside him. Ivan's eyes were open but he barely looked conscious.

"I let you down, Tzar Ivan."

"No, I let you down. Make that Mary pay for my death."

"I will, Ivan. I will," Szymon muttered as Ivan took his last breath.

Kurt approached and said, "It's ok, Szymon. You don't actually die in Hell. Your body disappears eventually, and you immediately re-spawn in the reception area of Limbo, where you have to talk to your case worker about why you died. Then you return to your circle of punishment."

"Oh. Well, that may be worse than death...but ok."

"I take it Mary escaped?"

"Yeah."

"Well, Ivan can get his revenge when he returns. We need to keep moving."

"How do we get out of here?"

"The boatman will take us." Kurt stared through the fog and yelled, "Phlegyas! Are you there, Phlegyas?"

A long rowboat appeared carrying a bulky, black and red magma golem with buffalo horns and a small crown upon his head.

"Sherghim. Can you please put us on that boat?"

Sherghim used their powers to move them to the boat, where Phlegyas rowed with a long oar.

"Greetings, Phlegyas," said Kurt.

Phlegyas nodded.

"Why are you here, Phlegyas?" asked Szymon.

"I burned down Apollo's temple after he raped

110

my virgin daughter."

"Punished for eternity for punishing a god for committing a sin? Hell is fucked."

"This place doesn't always make sense," added Kurt.

In the distance appeared a waterfall, which the boat and the sinners were heading straight toward. Demonic laughter sounded over the waves and the waterfall, as a gigantic black shadow creature appeared past the falls, its head far above the boat, long horns protruding from the temples.

"I see you've made it halfway, Szymon. I'm impressed."

"Lucifer! You will pay for putting me through this. I swear you will."

"Good, Szymon. Harness your rage. You will need it to get through the rest of Hell."

"Don't worry, I'll have plenty left over for you, big fella."

"Good, Szymon. Get angry."

"I see you can take any form, Lucifer, but I'm not afraid. The bigger they are, the harder they fall."

"Don't worry, Szymon. I can only take my true form in the 9th Circle."

"So, I must fight an angel? This will be fun."

"You'll see, Szymon. Soon enough."

"I look forward to it."

"Oh, and Kurt. I know you left Szymon unattended in Greed. Do your job as ordered or I will find you a new position. Perhaps bathing demons for eternity."

"Yes, your unholiness."

"Good. I will see you all soon."

Lucifer vanished as the boat reached the waterfall.

"Are we going down this waterfall?"

"It's the only way, Szymon," answered Kurt. "Hold on tight."

Szymon gripped the side of the boat as it tipped forward, pointing straight down the waterfall. The boat and its passengers plummeted down the waterfall as Sherghim floated safely away through the air. When the boat reached the river below, it hit the surface of the water and quickly righted itself.

"That wasn't so bad," said Szymon.

Ahead of them was a great city with high walls like a citadel. The walls and the towers on either side of the gate were a dull black, made from the same stone as the cave walls they had seen earlier in Hell. Standing on the black parapet, alongside the black gate, were 3 black-winged women with hideous faces and hair of black snakes, all wearing long black robes.

"Who's that?" asked Szymon.

"Those are the Furies, the sisters who guard the city Dis."

"We will not be granting you entrance to Dis, mortals," said Alecto in a high-pitch voice.

"But we WILL be tearing you limb from limb," added Tisiphone in a somewhat deeper voice.

"I want to eat their brains," said Megaera in an even deeper voice.

"Lucifer is expecting us. So you might as well let us in, ladies," said Kurt.

"We will be doing no such thing," the 3 sisters said in unison.

The sisters all took flight, each one flapping their blacks wings rhythmically to hover above where they had been standing.

"If we must dispatch you to gain entrance, that can be arranged," said Szymon.

"You think you can kill us?" asked Tisiphone incredulously.

"Well, yeah. I'm a professional." Szymon stood up in the center of the boat, holding his katana menacingly.

The Furies all laughed like cackling witches and

then flew toward the long rowboat. Immediately, an angel appeared in their way, bathed in white light and flapping their wings, the wind they created pushing back the Furies. The 3 sisters screeched and flew high above the city. The angel then held out their arms and released a glowing gold energy that shot forward, laying waste to the entire front wall of the citadel.

"You will let them through, you miserable wretches," the angel said with an echoing androgynous voice before leaving the way they came.

Chapter 10: Heresy

As Phlegyas' boat entered the city Dis, Szymon noticed that the River Styx WAS the street, and it was lined with flaming sarcophagi that were standing vertically. All that could be heard over the river was the crackling of the flames and the cries of the sinners.

"Welcome to the 6th Circle, fellas: Heresy."

"What are all the coffins for?" asked Szymon.

"Inside them are entombed the heretics."

"But aren't all the Pagans in Limbo?"

"Not quite. Limbo is simply for believers of something else. Heresy is reserved for disbelievers who preached against the church. Most these sarcophogi are empty though. Nobody commits this sin anymore."

"So who's here?"

"Galileo's here."

"The astronomer?"

"Yes, it was church law that the sun revolved around the Earth, so he was a heretic for claiming otherwise," answered Kurt.

"Wow. Just wow."

"I know."

"Who else?"

"Henry the Monk is here."

"Who?"

"Henry of Lausanne. He was against 2nd marriages and encouraged men to marry prostitutes to make them honest women."

"He sounds ok to me. If you ask me, neither of them deserves this punishment."

"Well, you said it yourself, Szymon. Hell is fucked."

Szymon lost it at hearing Kurt Vonnegut use the F word.

"Damn, Kurt. You feel strongly about this."

"I do. I'm lucky I'm not sentenced to an eternity in a flaming coffin."

"That's true. You weren't exactly a champion of Christianity."

"To say the least. I just feel that faith should be reserved for marriage or the weather. You have faith that your wife won't cheat on you. Or that it isn't going to snow. You don't have faith that this imaginary creature exists and not this other one. What do we actually know? Nothing. That's what."

At that moment, a group of black-cloaked individuals appeared. Each one approached a separate coffin and proceeded to urinate on them.

"What's this?" asked Sherghim.

"Those are the Satanists. It's their job to urinate on the flaming tombs. They are sinners too, but they are given a lighter punishment because they preached nothingness instead of another imaginary being."

"It's better to worship nothing than it is a cocker spaniel," added Sherghim.

"Oh yes, I heard about Nixmar," replied Kurt. "That is really too bad."

"Hold on. You thought a cocker spaniel was your god, but you visited Earth? Didn't you see a cocker spaniel on Earth?"

"We did, but we thought they were gods: relatives of our god. In fact, we thought all dogs and cats were gods because of how Humans treat them."

"That tracks. Makes complete sense. So what the Hell?" exclaimed Szymon. "These are the people in the 6th Circle? They don't deserve to be this deep in Hell."

"I agree, Szymon, but what can you do? Write a petition to God?"

"Once I defeat Lucifer, I will change this. I will change all of it."

"I have faith in you, Szymon."

"You do? I thought I had no chance of winning.

Remember what you said?"

"I remember what I said, but I have come to see how strong you are."

"You two get a room," interrupted Sherghim.

One of the satanists squatted to pee and Szymon yelled, "You! You're a female."

The satanist pushed back her hood and said, "Yes, Szymon. I still have a vagina."

The black-haired beauty with visible blonde roots smiled and Szymon slipped down the rabbit hole.

Szymon was 31. The year was 1989. He was sitting next to the black-haired woman on a brown and tan stripe-pattern sofa, wearing a black cloak over a shirt and pants. She wore a black Victorian dress with black fishnets on both her arms and her legs. They both watched Pink Floyd's The Wall on a large wooden television set sitting on the shag carpet of their apartment with a VCR on top of it.

"You feeling the acid yet, Szymon?"

"Yes, Becca, I think. My bedroom door is swallowing the carpet."

"No it's really doing that. We better get our money back."

"Shut up."

Szymon's brown hair hung to his chin, and his

eyes were bulging as he stared at Becca.

"You are so beautiful. Are you sure I'm gay?"

"Szymon, you are as queer as a 5-wheeled bicycle."

"Oh, shut up."

"No, seriously. Don't you dare confess your love to me like you did the last time we did acid."

"I don't love you. Well, actually I do. But, not like that."

"I love you too, Szymon. So, do you have the rent money? Sorry to ask right now, but I don't feel like being homeless. You know."

"Yeah, I have it. I killed a Saudi Arabian gun smuggler yesterday."

"Ha! One of these days you're gonna tell me what you do for a living, for real."

Becca began to convulse and fell on the floor, white foam pouring out of her mouth. Szymon called 911 and the medics from the New York Fire Department arrived, asking what drugs Becca had taken.

"Just acid. I think."

"Does she have any allergies?"

"Shitake mushrooms."

119

"Does she have any relatives in the city?"

"No."

"What religion is she?"

"She's a Satanist."

"She worships the devil?"

"No, she's a Satanist. She believes we're all responsible and accountable for our own shit."

"Oh, never heard of that. Well, sir. We would take you with to the hospital, but you're not a relative and you're on drugs. I advise you to wait near the phone and we'll call you with Rebecca's status as soon as we know it."

Szymon waited in a chair at the kitchen table, staring at the lime-green corded phone mounted to the wall that was plastered with vintage-firetruck print wallpaper. Szymon was listening to the sirens of the pictures of firetrucks when the phone rang. Szymon's heart beat like a jackhammer.

"Hello?" Szymon answered. "Yes, I'm Szymon."

Szymon listened to the woman speak and dropped the phone receiver. Falling to his knees and clenching his fists, Szymon screamed.

Szymon awoke from his daydream. He was still standing in the center of the boat holding his katana.

"It's good to see you, Szymon," said Becca.

"But you aren't a Satanist or a heretic."

"I'm going to kill Lucifer."

"Like you killed the Saudi Arabian?"

"Exactly like that."

"Good. I hear Satan's an asshole."

Szymon's eyes teared up and Kurt said, "Looks like we're already ready to leave this circle. See the chasm?"

Szymon looked ahead to see another waterfall, this one headed to the 7th Circle.

One of the men trapped in a burning coffin yelled, "There are only 3 real Star Wars movies!"

Sherghim lifted the 2 humans with their mind as Phlegyas turned the boat around.

"Farewell Phlegyas," said Kurt.

"Farewell Phlegyas," said Szymon.

"Farewell Phlegyas," said Sherghim.

Chapter 11: Violence

As the 3 sinners slowly descended into the chasm, Szymon noticed that the temperature had increased significantly. The water pouring into the chasm dissipated by evaporation as it went deep into the chasm. As the adventurers were lowered to the black riverbank below, they saw that The River Phlegethon was full of boiling blood instead of water. Countless sinners were wading in the wide blood river up to their chests or necks, and across it stretched a large bridge constructed from small black boulders. Scattered down the riverbanks were small fires. Standing guard along the river were centaurs with golden bows, ready to shoot sinners who tried to escape the blood.

"Welcome to the 7th Circle: Violence," said Kurt.

"Is that blood?"

"Yes, it's the blood of their victims. Very fitting punishment if you ask me."

"Definitely. So, are there 2 different punishments in this circle?"

As they began crossing the bridge, Kurt answered, "Actually, there are 3 rings. The outer ring is the violent toward others, the middle ring is the violent toward themselves, and the inner ring is the violent towards God."

"Oh, so I'll see Ernest in the middle ring. I hope

he's ok."

"If we can find him. There are a lot of suicide victims in Hell."

"Hey, is that Vlad the Impaler?" asked Szymon, looking at a tall man with long, curly black hair hanging beneath a burgundy hat encrusted with pearls.

"Count Dracula. In the flesh."

"Hey, who dares speak my name?"

"None of your business. What you gonna do? Suck my blood? Looks like you've got plenty of blood right there. You need a spoon? Or a ladle? How 'bout a straw?"

"You make jokes at me? Come say that to my face."

"Nah, I'd rather not."

"What an asshole," said Sherghim.

As the 3 sinners progressed across the bridge, Vlad called after them, "If you were real men, You'd say that close enough for me to kill you."

The many violent sinners looked like they would rip each other's throats out at any second if they weren't so busy writhing in agony from stewing in the boiling blood.

"Look, it's Aaron Kosminski," said Kurt, pointing at a man in his mid 20's with a mustache, wearing a 19th century black suit.

"Who?" asked Szymon.

"Jack the Ripper."

"Oh," said Szymon before calling, "Why'd you kill all those women, Jack? Can I call you Jack?"

"They weren't women. They were whores: servants of Satan. They were like rats spreading diseases. If rats had supple breasts and juicy vaginas."

"Wow."

"Yeah," said Kurt. "Definitely a creeper."

Far away, a blonde-haired man with glasses caught Szymon's eye.

"Holy shit, it's Jeffrey Dahmer."

"Yeah," replied Kurt, "I heard there's a new T.V. show about him. They've been talking about it in Limbo."

"Yeah, I don't watch T.V., but I hear the show both glorifies and humanizes Dahmer while sensationalizing his illness and the murders."

"It's pitiful what humans consider entertainment."

"Nixmarians are entertained by murderers. It's called the coloseum."

"Oh yeah. We had that on Earth 20 centuries

ago. Now we have the Ultimate Fighting Championship. Much less death, but just as entertaining." As Szymon spoke, he spotted a familiar face among the sinners wading in boiling blood.

"Father."

Szymon's father wore a gray cardigan sweater, his full head of shortish black hair disheveled. Szymon's face turned red as his mind slipped down the rabbit hole.

The year was 1979. Szymon was 21. He was wearing a black over-coat over his black suit, with black gloves on his hands and a black scarf around his neck. His hair was long and hung over his shoulders. Szymon was leaning against a tall Poplar tree, smoking a cigarette and watching a funeral from afar.

There was a white tent set up in front of the grave, where sat the casket on a lowering device. Under the tent were 3 rows of chairs where sat the closest relatives of the deceased, out of the wind and flurrying snow. The Rabbi said his closing prayer and the attendees began to disperse and/or mingle.

Szymon Sr. approached Szymon, quickly saying, "You have some fucking nerve showing your face here."

"He was my uncle. Why wouldn't I be here?"

Szymon pulled a flask from his coat pocket and took a long gulp.

"Since when do you smoke and drink?"

"Since none of your fucking business."

"It IS my business since you came from my testicles."

"Whatever you say, Dad."

"The police are still looking for you for killing your drill sergeant."

"So? Are you threatening to call them? Do it, and they'll be burying you next."

"Don't think I'm afraid of you just because you were trained by a samurai."

"What?"

"Yes, your mother told me everything. She can't hide anything from me. I won't let her."

"Did she tell you that Bernard raped me when I was 12?"

"Oh, drop the routine. Nobody raped you, and you know it. You're just making an excuse for being gay. And how dare you call my brother a faggot."

"See, that's why I didn't tell anyone: 'cause I didn't want people blaming a heinous crime for my sexual preference."

"The only heinous crime is your existence."

"I should kill you right now, while I have the

chance."

"With all these witnesses? Go ahead, Junior. Be my guest."

"I don't care about that. I'll end up in Gehenna some way or another. If it wasn't for Mom, you would have been the first to die. But she can't live without you, so consider yourself a lucky man. Saved by a woman's love."

"You WILL end up in Gehenna, Junior. And, when you get there, Bernard is going to get his revenge on you, you peter-puffing momma's boy. I'm leaving now. And, as soon as I find a payphone, I'm calling the cops."

"Good luck with that. I slashed your tires on the way in."

Szymon threw his cigarette butt on the ground and walked off.

That's when Szymon's mind returned to the 7th Circle. Szymon Sr. saw his son and said, "Hey, I know you. Where do I know you from?"

"It's me. Junior. You senile old fuck."

"Oh, my faggot son. How did you get so old? I was sure you'd get yourself killed a long time ago."

"That's because you don't know shit, Father."

"I'm surprised Bernard hasn't found you and killed your ass yet."

"You can't die in Hell, Father."

"Oh but you can. Over and over again. And he will never grow tired of getting his revenge."

"I was going to get my revenge on YOU, father. But it looks like Lucifer has you adequately fucked.

"On me? All I did was provide for you and your mother, and try to make you into a decent God-fearing man. But no, you had to be a pole-smoking cum dumpster."

"You were a God-fearing man, but look at you."

Kurt interrupted, saying, "Come Szymon. He's not worth the time."

When the adventurers made it across the bridge, they found an immense grove of trees and bushes shaped like people, growing from black soil. Upon the trees fed eagles with the heads and torsos of women.

"Are those harpies, Kurt?"

"Sure are, Szymon."

"Why are they eating the weird trees?"

"The trees are suicide victims who have been transformed."

"Oh damn." Szymon looked up to see many more harpies flying around above the grove, eating fireflies. They screeched, but not like eagles. It was more like women impersonating eagles. It was a hideous sound. "So I'm looking for a tree that resembles Ernest. Ernest! Are you here? Ernest McKenzie?"

Szymon got no response, so he continued to call out Ernest's name as he walked around through the grove. That's when Sherghim recognized a cluster of shrubs that were cube-shaped and were apparently Nixmarians.

"Meshtok! Vangor! Dujang! I am so sorry Stalnix did this to you. I will avenge you all when I find Stalnix. They should be in the 9th Circle. We are headed there now."

"You travel with Humans?" asked Vangor.

"Yes, they are good ones. You would like them. They are brave warriors with compassionate souls."

"Good," said Meshtok, "You must make Stalnix pay for this."

"Sorry to cut you short, Sherghim, but we really should chase after Szymon."

As they followed Szymon, Kurt said, "So, Sherghim, may I ask how they killed themselves?"

"Nixmarians possess the ability to self-detonate. We are basically immortal (impervious to illness, old age, and most injuries) so we self-detonate when we decide we have lived our best lives."

130

"Wow, that is truly fascinating."

The two caught up with Szymon, who was still calling out Ernest's name.

"I met Ernest Hemingway!"

"That's great Szymon. Wrong Ernest. But, how was he?"

"Very manly."

"No, I mean, how's he feel about being a tree and being eaten by harpies?"

"Not thrilled."

"To say the least, I'm sure. It's horrible that suicide is a sin. Let's punish people because the lives we gave them were too hard. Oh yeah, that makes sense," mocked Kurt.

"I agree wholeheartedly. At least homosexuality isn't really a sin. Didn't Dante say it was punished in the 7th Circle?"

"He did."

"Homosexuality a sin? That's the most absurd thing I've ever heard," said Sherghim.

"I agree," replied Szymon.

"I concur," added Kurt.

Szymon stepped away with his hands cupped around his mouth. "Ernest! Where are you, kiddo?"

131

yelled Szymon.

"Szymon, he may not be here," said Kurt, "Lucifer could have him trapped in the 9th circle with him."

"Shit, you're right. Well, I'll find him soon enough, one way or another."

"One way, or another, I'm gonna find ya. I'm gonna get ya, get ya, get ya, get ya!" sang a familiar voice to their right. Szymon turned to look and squealed like a schoolboy.

"Robin Williams!"

The gnarled Robin Williams-shaped tree moved its mouth to speak. "Nanu nanu."

"Mr. Williams, I'm so sorry you're here like this. You enriched so many lives. A just and merciful God would spare you this punishment."

"Be careful, he can hear you. And please. Call me Robin."

"Oh fuck God. He gave Lucifer reign over Hell. So it's his fault. Isn't he all-knowing? So he knows what goes on down here. And I'm sure he's noticed you're not in heaven putting him in stitches."

"I like your style. Who do I have the pleasure of speaking with?"

"Szymon Symanski. That is the novelist, Kurt Vonnegut, and Sherghim, 2nd heir of Nixmar."

132

"Pleasure. Put it there, pal. Oh I don't have hands. It's a travesty."

"Pleasure? The pleasure's all mine, I assure you. I've always looked up to you."

A harpy landed on top of Robin and began to eat him.

"Shoo," said Robin.

Szymon leaped forward and decapitated the bird-woman with his katana, the harpy falling to the ground in 2 pieces.

"Thank you, Szymon. I wish I could pay you to stand here and kill these ugly fuckers for me for the rest of time. We could talk about movies. And the San Francisco Giants. And gelato. I miss gelato."

"Sorry, I would do it for free, but I have to go kill Lucifer."

"Really? That sounds intriguing."

"It was nice meeting you, Robin," said Kurt, "Let's get moving, Szymon."

"It was so nice talking to you, Robin."

"Farewell," said Robin.

As the 3 travelers continued through the grove, Robin shouted, "Have fun storming the castle!"

As they walked/floated away, Szymon asked, "Wasn't that from Princess Bride? Robin wasn't in

133

that."

"No, it was Billy Crystal. They were close friends."

"Oh, that's right. Damnit Kurt. I wish I could save him."

"You can't save everyone, Szymon."

"Yeah, God couldn't even save the queen."

"You know who else God couldn't save?" asked one of the trees. "That goddamned Nixon."

Szymon turned and said, "Hunter S. Thompson! I swore it was the CIA that killed you."

"No, it was me, sadly. Just couldn't stand the state of the world anymore. Wish I had known I'd be a tree. Would have drunk more whiskey that night, so I could drink my own sap. What I wouldn't give for a good buzz. And a grapefruit."

"I can help with that," said Szymon, untying the sake bottle at his waist. He approached and fed Hunter a gulp of rice wine.

"Oh God that's good. I'm not a sake fan, but that is the nicest thing I have ever tasted."

"Glad you like it," Szymon said, sharing another gulp. "Don't know where it came from, just appeared when I got to Hell."

"Must be a gift from God. Have you seen Nixon?

134

He's gotta be here somewhere. I'd like to spit in his fat, grotesque face."

"I believe he's in the 9th Circle," replied Kurt, "For betraying his country."

"Ah, serves him right, the fucking scoundrel. If you see him, can you spit in his face? Tell him it's from me."

"Sure thing, Hunter."

"Let's keep moving, fellas," said Kurt. "Good to see you again, Hunter."

"Yes, as always. Keep subverting the system, boys."

As the 3 sinners walked/floated away, Hunter yelled, "Please! Tell me about the fucking golf shoes!"

"Oh, I love golf shoes," exclaimed Sherghim. "Taste like minsklats."

"Is that a fruit?"

"No, it is a rodent."

"Once again, you're a weird dude, Sherg."

"Thank you."

As they made progress through the enormous grove, a massive minotaur, wielding a double-edged axe appeared, charging at the adventurers.

"Oh shit," exclaimed the 3 in unison. They

turned and ran, and after a moment, Szymon looked back to see the minotaur gaining on them quickly.

"Fuck this," said Szymon, who stopped and turned with his katana ready to strike. When the beast saw Szymon's face, it came to a dead stop and began striking itself.

"Szymon," said Kurt, who had also stopped running, "It thinks you are Theseus, the man who killed it." Stepping forward, Kurt said, "That's right, Minotaur. I have brought Theseus to torture you for eternity."

The massive beast struck itself repeatedly with even greater force, and Kurt motioned for them to slip away as silently as possible. When they got past the minotaur, the grove opened up into a circular desert that was on fire. Spread throughout the flaming sands were the many heads of sinners who were buried neck deep. Among the heads were king crabs that were randomly pinching the heads of the sinners, who screamed in agony.

"This place is awful," said Szymon, who was scanning the desert for familiar faces.

"You're telling me," replied one of the blasphemers.

"George Carlin!"

"My man. How's it hangin?"

"It's an honor. I bought your album, Class Clown, when it came out, but my parent's confiscated it."

"They probably listened to '7 Words You Can't Say on Television' alone in their bedroom at night. I heard a lot of people were into that, before good porn was more readily available."

"That's hilarious. This sure is a heinous punishment for talking shit about God, don't you think?"

"Well, when you have such a big ego, it's easy to feel threatened. You think respect and reputation are human concepts? We were created in his image. That's all I'm saying."

"Hadn't thought of it like that."

"So what has you fellas walking around the 7th Circle?"

"Szymon here is challenging Lucifer for his throne," answered Kurt.

"Oh! Wish I could watch that. But it would be even better if it was God vs. Lucifer. I would trade my soul to see that. Oh! Lucifer owns my soul. Oh well."

One of the crabs headed toward George, and Szymon thrust his sword, stabbing the crab in the back. He stepped on the crab to pull his sword free and asked, "You want us to get you out of here?"

"Oh, no thanks. I hate to imagine what punishment I'll get for trying to escape. But, if you chop my head off, maybe I'll get to watch a little T.V. in

Limbo before I have to come back here."

"My pleasure, George."

"Have a nice break," said Kurt.

Szymon swung his katana low, chopping George's head clean off.

Kurt said, "Let's get the Hell out of here."

"Don't mind if we do."

The 3 approached the center of the desert, where opened up the next chasm, surrounded by a short wall like in Gluttony. As they neared the exit, Szymon skewered a few more crabs.

"Wish I had some boiling water. Crab legs in Hell. Just imagine."

Chapter 12: Fraud

After they descended the chasm at a safe speed, thanks to Sherghim's powers, Szymon noticed an infinite span of level black rock. Behind them was a black cave wall. In front of them was a black stone bridge that crossed a ditch. Past that bridge were other bridges. Szymon had no idea how many.

"Welcome to the 8th Circle," said Kurt.

"What's with the bridges," asked Szymon.

"There are 10 of them, each crossing one of the circular ditches that house the sinners, each boasting a different punishment for a different one of the 10 forms of fraud."

"Damn. That's a lot of sin. What's this one?"

As they crossed the first bridge, Kurt said, "This is the panderers and seducers."

The ditch was full of all sorts of people who were getting whipped by imps.

"Well, if the weakest punishment is an eternity of getting whipped, this should be fun."

Next, they crossed the second bridge, and Kurt said, "This is the excessive flatterers."

The sinners were buried in elephant dung up to the neck, and one of the flatterers yelled to Szymon, "I really like your hair, sir. You must have a very expensive stylist. Are you an actor?"

"How pathetic."

"Indeed."

"Indeed."

When they crossed the 3rd bridge, Kurt said, "These are the simonists."

"The what?"

"People who sold church offices or holy relics."

"Oh, I guess that's not cool."

"Not really."

The simonists were buried upside down in holes as deep as them, so that their feet were at the surface, being burned by the flaming embers coating the floor of the ditch.

The next ditch was full of people with their heads twisted completely backwards, walking around backwards for the rest of time. As they crossed the bridge, Szymon said, "That's weird."

"These are the soothsayers."

"But what about the fortune teller? Why was she in Greed instead of here?

"I don't know, Szymon. Maybe it was decided that greed was her greatest sin."

"Oh, is that how it works?"

"Sometimes."

Next, they crossed the 5th bridge, where sinners were immersed in boiling pitch.

"Who are these?"

"These are the grafters."

"Like grifters?"

"Correct."

"Oh, I was grifted once. 3 Card Monty. Never again. Fuck grifters."

The next ditch contained sinners walking around, wearing heavy gold-painted robes made of lead. "These are the hypocrites," said Kurt as they crossed the bridge.

"Wow, that's a sin? I always felt like everyone was a hypocrite."

One of the sinners yelled, "You damn hypocrites! You all deserve to wear those heavy robes."

Szymon laughed.

As they crossed the next bridge, Kurt said, "These are the thieves."

The sinners walked around inside the ditch with their hands tied behind their backs with snakes. Their heads had all been metamorphosed into something hideous. Monstrous even.

141

"That's a weak punishment."

"Yeah, I don't know if I agree with the order of these punishments myself," Kurt replied.

"No, these are not in the right order," agreed Sherghim.

The next ditch was full of sinners covered in tree sap and entirely wrapped in flames.

"Now, that's a punishment. What's it for?"

"These are the deceivers," answered Kurt as they crossed the 8th bridge. "Look, it's Tammy Faye Bakker. Or I guess it's Messner now."

Tammy Faye's big blonde hair and hoop earrings were dead giveaways.

"Oh shit, it is. Good for her. After taking advantage of all those desperate people. Now this I agree with, 'cause that's what you get for selling God."

"I don't disagree with you at all, Szymon." As they reached the 9th bridge, Kurt said, "These are the scandalous."

The sinners in the 9th ditch were naked and were being mutilated with short swords by many imps.

"Well, that looks unpleasant."

The 10th ditch was full of sinners, some of which were scratching themselves feverishly, some of which looked very ill, and the rest of which were begging for water.

"These are the forgers," said Kurt. "The forgers of metals have scabies. The forgers of words have deadly fevers. And the forgers of money are suffering from deadly thirst."

One of the sinners begging for water was an incredibly large, obese man with greasy black hair combed over his bald pate.

"That's Marco Ferrari, the Italian counterfeiter I killed 20 years ago."

That's when Szymon slipped down the rabbit hole.

The year was 2003. Szymon was 45. He was wearing a white shirt and black slacks with a black apron tied around his waist. He held a tray holding 6 pieces of tiramisu on separate plates and a cup of coffee. With his other hand, he spun the lid off a small, plastic bottle with his thumb and poured laxative into the coffee and tossed the bottle on the ground. That's when he exited the kitchen and approached the only table in the restaurant that was seated.

There were 6 mobsters in gray or black suits, discussing business. Szymon handed out all the desserts and set the coffee in front of Marco. He then exited and tucked himself away in the bathroom, in one of the 3 stalls.

That was when Marco entered in a hurry and went into the first stall. He heaved and panted, and

Szymon slipped out and kicked in the first stall door, with a pistol with a silencer on it in his right hand. He shot the fat man thrice in the heart, but he lunged at Szymon, his pants still around his ankles. Marco struck Szymon so hard he flew back into a sink, breaking it off the wall entirely. Marco pulled his pants up and fastened them, bent over from exhaustion and panting like a pit bull.

"I will eat YOU for dessert."

Szymon felt a sharp pain in his back where he had struck the sink, but he stood quickly and used his strength to pick the sink up over his head and slam it down on Marco's head. That was when Szymon picked up his gun, climbed out the bathroom window, and ran down the alley, holding his back.

Szymon woke from his daydream and Marco said, "You. You put me here. Give me something to drink. You owe me."

"I don't owe you shit. You fucked up my spine. You owe me for doctor bills."

Just past the last bridge was the chasm heading to the 9th Circle. As they peered into the large hole, Szymon said, "Ready or not, Lucifer, here I come."

Chapter 13: Treachery

As Shergim lowered Szymon and Kurt into the 9th Circle, Szymon noticed the "ground" was in fact a frozen lake. Behind them was a black cave wall and in front of them a good ways were tremendous black, stone pillars that went up all the way to the top of the massive cavern. Far in the distance was a structure made of black stone.

"Welcome to Treachery," said Kurt. "You see the pillars? They separate the 1st ring from the 2nd, and the next row separates the 2nd from the 3rd. First are those who betrayed their family. Next are those who betrayed their country. Then, are those who betrayed their guests. And, finally, are those who betrayed God."

The sinners were frozen in the lake, those in the first ring frozen up to their waists.

"So my uncle is in the first ring. I hope you guys don't mind, but I must find him."

"Szymon, Bernard isn't in the 1st ring. He's in the 4th with Lucifer."

"He betrayed God? What the Hell?"

"Not quite. I'll explain when we get there."

"Ok, now you've got me on edge."

"Sorry, Szymon. It will all make sense soon."

"Ok, let's get this over with."

The 3 began moving forward, passing many sinners trapped in the ice.

"I really expected a more severe punishment than this. The people buried in dung have it worse than this. And the people buried upside down with their feet on fire."

"I agree, Szymon. But there's no use arguing with supreme beings."

"I get that."

That was when Szymon noticed Ernest frozen in the lake with the other sinners.

"Ernest! What are you doing here? I looked for you in the ring of suicides but you were here. Why?"

"I'm not what you think, Szymon. I may be young, but I'm not innocent. I murdered my parents."

"What? Why?"

"They forgot my birthday. I mean I knew I wasn't going to get the car I asked for, but they didn't even remember to cook me lobster and invite my aunts and uncles."

"Aren't you a spoiled brat?"

"How dare you! I killed myself for you. I did you a huge favor, and you ended up here anyway. Hold up. Why aren't you being punished?"

"I came here to...defeat Lucifer and take his

throne."

"Damn, I didn't take you as the ambitious type."

"Can't judge a book by its cover, can you, Ernest?"

"Fair enough."

"God, I wish I had never met you."

"Hey, that's not very nice. Wait. You came here to rescue me, didn't you? And now you're pissed cuz I'm a murderer."

"No."

"Yes. But that's hypocrisy, because you're a murderer."

"I'm a hit-man."

"Tomatoes, potatoes. Whatever, Szymon. I don't want your help anyway. I deserve this punishment."

"At least you realize that."

"You bore me. Don't you have a devil to kill?"

"Farewell forever, Ernest."

Szymon walked off, and the other 2 followed. Kurt said, "I'm sorry, Szymon. That's gotta be tough, finding out you came all this way for nothing. What will you do now?"

147

"I will defeat Lucifer."

"You're still going to fight him?"

"Of course. I'm going to revamp Hell when I'm the Prince of Darkness. This place is a mess."

"I commend you for that decision, Szymon. It would be an honor to work for you."

"Don't worry, Kurt. I will find you a better job."

"You don't have to do that."

"It's no trouble. Really."

"Well, first you have to win."

They reached the first set of pillars as Szymon replied, "Just leave that up to me."

Szymon's mind was a live embryo immersed in boiling water. "I can't believe I misjudged him so poorly," thought Szymon. "I gave up everything. But everything happens for a reason. I'll make this a better place, I swear."

At that moment, Sherghim suddenly rose 100 feet in the air and plummeted at a great speed, smashing into the ice.

"Stalnix!"

Ahead of them was a nixmarian half frozen in the lake. They were a darker green than Sherghim.

"I know you are here for revenge but, if you kill

me, I will only shortly return to my punishment."

"That is why I will follow you and kill you over and over again until the end of time. You will have to spend an eternity with me. Dying."

"Fine. Then let it begin."

"Farewell, my friends," Sherghim said to Kurt and Szymon.

"Farewell, Sherghim."

Catch ya later, Sherg."

Sherghim rose up a hundred feet again and slammed into the ice. Then he zipped forward and, when he was next to Stalnix, Sherghim exploded, both Nixmarians sending off fragments of green gelatin in all directions.

"They will be missed."

"They're gonna give that fucker Hell."

"Shall we?"

"Let's do this."

They continued walking, and Szymon thought, "And to think, I hated that dude at first. Now I miss them. Already. Who's gonna talk about eating socks and rodents? And about worshiping a cocker spaniel?"

"You ok, Szymon?"

"Yeah, just thinking."

149

"About Sherghim? Yeah, me to. They were a great help."

"Have pretty useful powers."

"Yeah. Pretty useful."

As they walked through the 2nd ring, they did not see Richard Nixon, and Szymon felt bad they could not fulfill Hunter S. Thompson's final wish. Shortly after they passed the 2nd set of pillars, Szymon spotted Adolf Hitler, frozen up to his neck like all the sinners in this ring.

"Holy fuck. Look who it is, Kurt."

"Only the least popular man in history."

"At least I get to spit on SOMEone. Hold on, this is betrayal of guests. What guests did Hitler betray?"

"The Jewish people."

"Oh. Damn right he did."

Szymon approached Hitler, coughed up all the phlegm he could, and spit right as Hitler began to speak. The spit landed in his mouth and Szymon shouted, "Choke on that, you vile piece of shit!"

As they continued walking toward the black structure, which could now be seen as a palace of sorts, Szymon said, "God, that felt good."

"Your mother would be proud."

The black palace was made from the same stone that made up the cave walls. It had 6 pillars in the front and 6 giant gargoyles carved 3 stories above the surface of the lake. The front door was also stone and was guarded by 2 imps holding halberds. When Kurt and Szymon approached, the imps looked alarmed.

"Who approaches?" asked the 1st imp.

"Kurt Vonnegut. I bring Szymon Symanski to challenge the dark prince for his throne."

"Well, he's gonna lose, dumbass," said the 2nd imp.

"We'll see about that," replied Szymon.

Szymon hefted the large, black door open, and inside was a large foyer with a wrap-around staircase coming down on both the right and left sides of the foyer. Beneath the stairs, in the center of the wall, was an elevator. The floor was the frozen lake, and in the center of the foyer were two familiar sinners trapped entirely in the ice. The first was Judas Iscariot. The second was a fallen angel with black wings and horns.

"Lucifer? How am I supposed to fight him if he's frozen in ice?"

"You're not," said a man appearing to be in his 40s, descending the staircase wearing army fatigues and a VFW shirt.

"Bernard!"

"Szymon. Oh how I've waited for this moment. For 44 years I've thought about what I'd say to you. Frankly, I thought you'd be here sooner, but it's fine. I enjoy ruling Hell."

"You defeated Lucifer?"

"I did. And he was a pushover. I fought gooks in the war that were harder to best."

"So that was you this whole time? You were Sammy Davis Jr? That was a good impression. And I always thought you weren't good at anything."

"Weren't good at anything? I was the greatest soldier the Army ever had."

That was when Szymon slipped down the rabbit hole. The year was 1970. Szymon was 12. He was sitting next to Bernard on an orange sofa. Bernard was well-built but wasn't a large man. His hair was cropped short and he wore a black eye patch over his left eye.

Bernard's living room was decorated with framed medals and other war memorabilia. Szymon was staring at his uncle's purple heart.

"What did you do to earn that one, Uncle Bernie?"

"Oh that? Nothing special. Took a piece of shrapnel to the eye. Doctor said I was lucky to survive, but I don't believe in luck. Hey, you want some peppermint schnapps, Junior? It's really good.

"I'm not supposed to drink."

"It's ok. It will be our little secret."

"O.K."

When Bernard poured Szymon's glass, he dropped a pill in the schnapps and waited for it to dissolve before returning to the living room.

"Bottoms up, Junior."

Szymon swallowed a gulp and coughed.

"It's good, huh? Put hair on your chest."

Once Szymon had finished most the glass, he felt quite a buzz, his entire body numb, and his head extremely warm.

"You wanna make 50 bucks, Junior."

"What do I have to do?" asked Szymon, his speech slurred. Szymon dropped his glass on the carpet. He was no longer able to move his body.

"All you have to do is get a really good blowjob. I bet you have a monster cock."

Szymon giggled as his head, which he could no longer hold up, rested on his shoulder.

As Bernard unzipped Szymon's pants, Szymon blacked out. When he came to, his pants were zipped up and he held 15 dollars in his right hand.

That's when Szymon slipped back to the 9th

Circle.

"Fuck you, and fuck your revenge, Bernard. You can't get revenge on someone for getting revenge on you. Makes no sense. Anyway, I'm going to kill you again, and this time I'm taking your throne."

"The mouth on this kid. Thanks for your help, Kurt, but you can return to Limbo now."

"No thanks, your majesty. I'm going to stay with Szymon until he's completed his quest."

"Don't get mouthy with me."

Bernard pointed at Kurt, and he vanished completely.

"If you have supreme powers, why don't you just freeze me in this ice?"

"What fun would that be? So, are you going to formally challenge me, Junior?"

"Oh, uh, yeah. I challenge you for your throne, you lecherous fuck."

"Good, let's get it over with."

Bernard motioned for Szymon to join him, and the elevator opened, playing God-awful music. They both entered, and the door closed.

"Don't think about attacking me. My powers are limitless here. During the challenge, I must turn the Lucifer powers off. So you might have a chance."

154

"Don't worry, I'm not into treachery anyway."

The door opened and the 2 exited in the center of a coliseum. It appeared they were on the roof of the palace. The seats were all empty. Bernard snapped his fingers and suddenly the coliseum was full of imps and an assortment of greater and lesser demons. The din was quite loud. The elevator disappeared, and between Szymon and Bernard appeared an imp with a red cloth.

"Choose your weapon, Szymon," Bernard said as he gestured toward a long weapon rack holding everything from clubs to ray-guns.

Szymon drew his katana, the aura glowing a darker blue than before. Bernard was handed an antique M-1 Carbine semi-automatic rifle by an imp, and he snapped his fingers, apparently becoming mortal.

The imp in the center of the arena spoke into a microphone, "Ladies and gentle-demons. In this corner is the challenger, Szymon Szymanski."

All the demons booed and hissed.

"And in this corner is the champion, Bernard Szymanski."

All the demons cheered and whistled.

The imp raised the cloth in the air, waited a few seconds, and dropped it on the ground. Bernard pulled the trigger, firing several rounds, and Szymon

155

sprinted to his left as the bullets sent black dust into the air. Szymon turned and charged towards his uncle. Bernard let off a 3 round burst and Szymon sliced diagonally through the air with his sword, cutting 2 of the bullets in half. The 3rd bullet pierced Szymon's left arm, leaving a red hole in his kimono. The demons in the stands booed loudly.

"Nice show, nephew."

Bernard dropped the rifle and pulled a ka-bar (Marine issue knife) from his boot. As Szymon neared, preparing to swing, Bernard lunged low, quickly slicing Szymon's thigh with his knife. Szymon turned and swung, but Bernard did a somersault out of the way. That was when Bernard ran and picked up the M-1, pulling a loaded clip from his pocket and reloading the rifle. Szymon charged him at full speed but he wasn't quick enough. Bernard hit Szymon with 3 rounds in the arm, chest, and leg. Szymon collapsed on the ground. Bernard dropped the semi-automatic rifle once again, picking up his ka-bar and approaching Szymon to make sure he was dead. The demons in the stands went wild, cheering raucously.

When he reached Szymon, Bernard rolled him over and Szymon said, "You still owe me 35 bucks." On the ground next to Szymon was a live grenade.

"No fucking way!"

Kaboom!

Szymon woke up on the floor of an elevator. Godawful music was playing from a speaker. As he

156

stood, the door opened. Kurt Vonnegut was standing on the other side of the door, in the middle of the red waiting room in Limbo.

"Welcome back, your majesty. Is there anything I can get you?"

Szymon smiled and asked, "You got triple mocha frapuccino in this joint? And how about an ostrich egg? Over medium of course."

"You can create those with your new powers, Szymon. So I was wondering what you will be doing with your uncle."

"I've decided that, from now on, rapists will be punished by having their genitals nicked with razor blades dipped in lemon juice."

Szymon snapped his fingers, grinning vehemently.

Made in the USA
Monee, IL
19 July 2023

39591388R00089